Murder at Kangaroo Downs

June Whyte

A Vets2U Mystery

Book 1

White City

Press

Books by June Whyte

Sex on Tuesdays

THE GUMSHOE CHICK MYSTERY SERIES
Gone to the Dogs
For the Love of Dogs
Doggone It!

VETS 2U MYSTERY SERIES
Murder at Kangaroo Downs
Death at Dingo Creek
Homicide at Emu Lodge

KAT MCKINLEY GREYHOUND MYSTERIES
Chasing Can Be Murder
Muzzled
Hounded
Leashed

CHIANA RYAN CHILDREN'S MYSTERIES
The Case of the Disappearing Corpse
The Case of the Missing Dinosaur Egg

www.amazon.com/author/junewhytebooks

Murder at Kangaroo Downs

June Whyte

This edition published by White City Press
An imprint of Misti Media LLC
https://www.mistimedia.com
Available in both Paperback and eBook Editions
1 2 3 4 5 6 7 8 9 10
Text Copyright © June Whyte 2017
Cover design by *GetCovers*
Paperback ISBN: 9781963479157
eBook ISBN: 9781963479058

To my husband, Jim—the boxing butcher boy ☺

Acknowledgements

No author writes in a vacuum. Over the last few years I've had a lot of advice, cyber butt-kicks and loving hugs from Robyn, Wendy and Marg. Hey, if it wasn't for you three, instead of sitting in my socks at the computer with a coffee and a biscuit in hand—I'd be back training greyhounds and dashing around in all that sun and rain. I'd also like to thank my amazing cover artist, Annie Moril at http://anniemoril.com.

1

Kicking Peter to the Curb

"Can you feel the other testicle, doc?"

Dr. Emily Harrison B.V.Sc (Hons) smiled at the burly man with the anxious crease furrowed between his eyes, whipped off her latex gloves and tossed them in the direction of the waste bin.

"Sure can, Jack. It's up high. In the abdomen." She studied the man's craggy face, toughened to leather by his sixty-odd Australian summers. "Of course you know we can't leave it there."

He let out a long drawn out sigh and wrinkled his nose in distaste.

"Could turn cancerous if left any longer," she urged.

"Yeah, yeah, I know." Two red spots highlighted the man's otherwise sun-tanned cheeks. He looked down at his scuffed work boots and when he spoke there was still a trace of doubt in his voice. "Will the operation hurt?"

Emily grinned at him. "That's why a guy called William Morton invented general anesthetic way back in 1846."

He looked up, blinked a couple of times as though digesting and classifying this new data, then let out a loud guffaw. "You're a real card, doc. Okay, my horse deserves a stud career when he finishes racing so go ahead and schedule an appointment for next week."

"You're doing the right thing, Jack." Emily patted her equine patient's sleek chestnut neck, smiled into his large trusting eyes and reached up to gently pull on one soft ear. Then, straightening, she shook her head at the horse's owner. "It's no wonder the poor guy hasn't been stretching out in his last few races, the undescended testis pinches him at full stretch so he slows down." She paused. "Put yourself in his place."

"Um…think I might give that one a miss thanks, doc."

Emily laughed, undid the big chestnut stallion from the tie-up ring and handed his lead rope to Jack. "Okay, get your off-sider, Blue, to load this fellow back in the float while you and I see what day next week we can schedule High Stake's op."

The moment Emily entered the Equine clinic's large reception area, she knew *he* was there. Peter. She came to a sudden halt and narrowed her eyes, the all too familiar reek of Brut almost choking her. From behind the horse-shoe counter stepped a long-legged male, dressed in a white vet coat over blue shirt and jeans, that little boy twist of guilt she knew so well puckering his lips. A tidal wave of anger smashed into Emily's chest and if Jack Tremaine hadn't been following her into the room she'd have kneed her cheating husband in the groin and hopefully propelled *his* testis up into *his* abdomen.

"What the hell are *you* doing here, Peter?"

"Hey, thought you might need a hand, babe. You know, seeing it's your last day at the clinic." He gave her his well-practiced puppy-dog look. The one he used to wriggle out of every scrape he'd landed in since the day, aged five, when caught nicking a chocolate frog from the local deli. And now, thirty-three years later, all it did was make Emily want to deck him.

"Well you thought wrong," she told him through gritted teeth. Her fists clenched the patient's file so tightly the cardboard creased. How did she ever imagine this man was her soul-mate? Over the last six months she'd had suspicions he'd been playing around but hadn't allowed herself to believe it. Not until the day she'd gone hunting through the bottom of his wardrobe for his 'lucky' socks so she could wash them ready for their appointment with the bank manager. Instead, she'd found a small collection of panties. And they weren't hers. Not only had Peter been operating on race horses, he'd also been operating on their female handlers and collecting panties for keepsakes.

"Emily—"

"I'll see you in the divorce court, Peter, and you'd better have a good lawyer because I'm going to screw you like you've been screwing every female client who's ever walked through the door of our clinic." Her anger on a tight leash, she snapped a look at High Stakes' open-mouthed owner and let out a sharp breath. The poor man stood awkwardly shifting from one foot to the other. "Sorry, Jack," she said. "You'll have to get Peter to book your horse in for surgery. I have to go. The stink of cheating pig in here is overpowering. All the best for the future and I hope the operation results in your stallion winning heaps of races for you."

Peter took a step in her direction. "Emily, there's no need to…"

Arrrgh.

A widening crack threatened to let her self-control loose from its cage. Hands shaking, she snarled and dragged a metal chair toward her. Immediately both men scuttled backwards, Peter almost falling over his feet in his hurry to get out of range. Emily took a deep breath, closed her eyes and counted to ten. If she didn't walk out of the door right now, out of this profitable equine clinic where she'd spent the last eight years in partnership with her double-crossing, adulterous, two-timing husband, God knows, she'd wrap the chair around his head and probably end the day in jail.

"Anyone for a cup of java?"

Sally? Sally Packer? No. It couldn't be. Emily's teeth bit into her bottom lip to physically stop from screaming. Sally wasn't supposed to be in today either. This was turning into a Fawlty Towers farce. The bright purple thong she'd found sitting in pride of place on top of Peter's trophy collection belonged to their nurse receptionist and her supposed friend, Sally Packer. The same La Perla designer thong Emily had splurged a hundred dollars on so Sally would have a sexy surprise for her fiancé on the night of her engagement party two months ago.

As it turned out the surprise was on her.

The metal chair bounced off the tiled floor, scattering piles of colorful leg wraps and plastic halters stacked against the waiting room wall and landed at Peter's feet. Then, satisfied with the sudden jolt of fear flickering in his eyes, Emily snatched her tote bag from under the reception desk and stormed from the clinic. If she ever saw her cheating, soon-to-be ex-husband again, it would be in her dreams—he'd have his head on a chopping block and she'd be the one holding the axe.

2

Garfield on Steroids

Emily flung her bag onto the passenger seat of her little red Toyota Echo and jammed the key into the ignition. She had to get away. Anger bubbled in her stomach like a stew set on the stove to simmer. She let out a string of four letter words, all beginning with the letter F, and screeched from the private parking lot nestled beside the equine vet clinic's stable block. Once on the roadway, she ducked and dived from lane to lane. It suddenly seemed imperative that she get as far away and as fast as she could from the man who'd turned her life into a bad soapie—with Emily starring as the clichéd cuckolded wife.

It took a close call with a 28-wheeler road train and an angry shout from the tattooed driver, to finally bring Emily to her senses. Hands shaking, she pulled the car over into the next siding and slumped forward, head resting on the steering wheel. Why did she continually let Peter get to her like this? It was unproductive. She took a deep breath, held it for a count of eight, like she'd read in a yoga magazine at a dentist's waiting room, closed her eyes and let her breath out slowly, imagining her angry thoughts scattering like the petals of a rose in a strong wind.

Ommmmmmmmm…let good thoughts fill body and mind. Now close the door on the old life and see another door opening.

In her mind Emily projected a picture of the bright fuchsia colored door on the houseboat she'd purchased two days after she'd discovered

Peter's panty stash, from a guy who was relocating to England. A pink door with the words: '*Dr. Emily Harrison BVSc (Hon)—Vets2U—Mobile veterinary practice*', on a brass plaque across the front. She'd borrowed money from the bank to pay for the boat, figuring once her divorce settlement came through she could repay the loan in full. After all, the money from half of the house and their prosperous Equine veterinary clinic would leave her well off. As well as pony clubbers and pleasure horses, sleek, well-bred thoroughbreds, harness horses, Olympic showjumpers and eventers passed through their doors for treatment.

At the thought of her boat, Emily opened her eyes and smiled, body fully relaxed. She loved everything about her floating home, especially the miniature office she'd set up to run her new business. The office was tucked away in a narrow space between the warm chocolate colored leather lounge in the sitting area and the wood-paneled bar adjoining the small galley. Already she'd had the name of the boat changed from *Daisy 3* to *Vets2U*, which she'd had painted in large black letters on both sides of the hull and with the full-page advertisement she'd inserted in all the racing papers and several popular equine and canine magazines, Emily couldn't wait to take on her first assignment. All she needed now was a new van for transport and another vet, or even a qualified assistant to make her mobile-vet business complete. And she had several well-credentialed applicants to interview for that job in the morning.

A tinny rendition of Taylor's Swift's *Love Story* brought her out of her reverie. She hastily dug in the depths of her tote and scrabbled around for her phone, deciding with a deep-throated growl that it was way past time she changed her ringtone to Neil Diamond's *Love on the Rocks*. She checked caller ID. Good. It wasn't Peter. She put the phone to her ear. "Yes."

"And a good afternoon to you too," a familiar honey-sweet voice drawled.

"Maggie?" she screamed. "Maggie Post? Where are you? Where've you been?"

Last time Emily had heard from her sister-in-law and best friend was at Maggie's husband's funeral, three months ago. After the service Maggie had disappeared, leaving only a cryptic note telling everyone she'd put her property on the market, taken her daughter out of school and moved to some mystery cottage in the middle of god-knows-where. The only conclusion Emily could come up with was that Maggie was grieving for her husband, Lieutenant Sergeant Greg Post, who'd been killed in a police drug bust gone wrong—and she wanted to grieve alone.

But three months without contact?

"I'll fill you in when I see you, okay?" said Maggie. "Emily, sweetie, is there any chance of picking me up from Tolley Reserve? It's a couple of ks from your clinic?"

"I know where the park is, Mags. But what are *you* doing there?"

"Long story—short version—I was on the way to see you and Peter and my car broke down. Think I forgot to check the water before I left from Burra this morning."

A laugh bubbled up in Emily's chest. Her sister-in-law had a history of treating cars like throwaway cardboard boxes. "Of course I'll come and pick you up, Mags. Where exactly in the park are you?"

"Find my car and you'll find me."

"Okay. I'll be there in five," Emily said and tossed her phone onto the seat beside her.

Traffic was heavy when she pulled back out onto the main highway, so at the next set of lights she steered her Echo onto a quieter road and set off along the back streets toward Tolley Reserve, a popular picnic spot for locals and tourists. Had Maggie been living in Burra for the last three months—a mere hour and a quarter drive away? Or had that just been a stop-over on the way from wherever she'd been hiding? And why hadn't Maggie contacted her during that time? They'd been best friends from childhood. Emily would have been there for her, supported her in her loss and Maggie knew that. It still hurt to think Peter's sister, her sister-in-law, her best friend, had taken off without a word.

Emily drove slowly along the length of the park, eyes peeled for signs of Maggie or her broken-down car. Last time she'd seen Maggie she'd been driving a battle-scarred jeep which was perfect for someone who lived on a large property, bred thoroughbred horses and made the occasional veterinary call-out to treat a friend's dog that had been kicked by a recalcitrant bull, a neighbor's horse caught up on a barbed wire fence or a nearby farmer's lamb or calf that refused to leave its mother's womb. No jeep in sight—probably forgot to put water in that one too—only a dusty white Ford station wagon on the side of the road, hood up, smoke rising from under the bonnet.

Slowing down, Emily noticed a woman, plump, dark hair gathered in an untidy bun, hunched over on a park bench, her head down between her knees as though she was ill.

Maggie?

Emily jammed her foot on the brake, switched off the engine and almost tripped as she threw herself out of the car and ran toward the woman.

"What happened, Mags?" she said, her breath coming out in gasps as she tried to come to terms with her long-lost friend in trouble. Again. "Are you hurt? Were you attacked by muggers? Do you want me to call an ambulance?"

The woman hunkered over on the park bench glanced up. "Aah, just in time," she said, sliding off the bench onto one knee. "I'm trying to get this blasted drain up and it's stuck. There's a cat trapped underneath. Must have crawled in somewhere else and couldn't find his way out again." She looked up with a rueful smile. "Any chance of rolling up your sleeves and giving me a hand here, Em?"

"Like old times, hey?" Emily grinned then leant forward to peer down through the metal grate at her feet. In the drain below, a cat the size of a baby tiger, one ear ripped, eyes crossed, so ugly he'd make cane toads look beautiful, hissed and spat his disdain at their tardiness in rescuing him.

"Looks a bit cranky, doesn't he?" Emily bent to give the drain a tug. As Maggie said, the drain was stuck like a tick to a dog's back. "Hang on." She stood up. "There's a tire lever in the boot of my car. Might do the trick."

Even using their combined strength, plus the tire lever, it took another ten minutes of grunting and cursing before the drain finally flipped open with a loud crash. Out sprang Garfield on Steroids. The giant tom-cat glared balefully at his rescuers, gave a quick body shake and then stalked off along the path, probably intent on rustling up a couple of baby birds for lunch.

"Any time," said Maggie to the feral tom's retreating back.

"Enjoy the rest of your day," added Emily.

And with that they both doubled over, laughing.

"Oh God, the look on his face…" Maggie dropped onto the bench and held her stomach.

"Face? More like a squashed pie!" Emily spluttered.

Giggling like a schoolgirl, Emily helped Maggie to her feet. She'd forgotten how the smallest joke or innuendo could set them both off. Ever since they'd met in primary school they'd been the same. "Come on, Mags," said Emily. "Let's go get a coffee and you can tell me how much chocolate and ice cream you've been stuffing into yourself over the last three months."

"How'd you guess?"

"'Cos that's what you do every time life gets hard. Run away and eat chocolate. I remember when that skinny kid with the buck teeth wouldn't be your milk-partner in fifth grade. What was his name? Twister? Clinker? No…Splinter, that's right. When I went looking for you, I found you hiding under a bush scoffing a big box of Roses chocolates your mum had bought for you to give me for my birthday, so I crawled under the bush and helped finish off the box."

"Yeah."

"And remember in seventh grade when you didn't get picked for the netball team after you'd come to every practice—you ate your way through two cartons of chocolate fudge ice cream and puked up on your mum's new carpet?"

Maggie poked out her tongue. "Okay, okay, you've made your point."

And then Emily watched as her friend's shoulders sagged. "But this time it was different." Maggie's voice was so soft Emily had to lean closer. "*This* time I had to get through on my own. *This* time it was the love of my life and…and I had to come to terms with the fact that Greg…Greg's not coming back." She grabbed a quick breath and let it out slowly.

"I know, Mags," said Emily watching her friend's bottom lip quiver. "I know." Emily choked back a sob. No wonder Maggie had opted out of the world after her husband was killed. They'd been soul mates from the first time they'd met, when Greg, the cop, picked up Maggie, the vet, for not wearing a seatbelt when coming home from a difficult calving, late one night. After issuing her with a ticket, he'd asked her out on a date. And Maggie had gone. They'd been married three months later.

Swallowing the lump in her throat Emily held out both arms. "Come here, Mags."

Maggie walked into Emily's arms and burrowed her head in her shoulder. "It still seems unreal," she said, her voice muffled. "I keep expecting Greg to walk in the door, pick me up and twirl me around. He'd always spin me around until I squealed, then he'd laugh and kiss me fair on the mouth."

"I know, Mags. Just take it one day at a time. I'm here for you."

"Thanks, Em." Maggie stepped back and wiped her eyes with the back of her hand. "You always have been."

Plastering a smile on her face, Emily linked arms with Maggie and headed in the direction of her car. "Now…let's go grab that coffee. Don't know about you, but I'm parched. Rescuing giant cats sure leaves you with a giant thirst!"

3

Convincing Maggie

Five minutes later, Emily angled her little red Echo into a vacant space in the car park at Café Aqua, a family restaurant on the outskirts of town.

"Hmm…bit crowded," she said, "but they do make a top cappuccino." She turned off the motor and stretched the kinks from her neck and shoulders. Throwing chairs at cheating husbands and rescuing ungrateful cats tended to have unhealthy side effects—like sore stiff muscles, aching shoulders and brain fog. Who'd have thought? As Emily ran her fingers through her short blonde hair she caught a glimpse of her face in the rear vision mirror and let out a small shriek. There was dirt on her left cheek bone and her hair stood on end. She dug out a tissue and scrubbed at her left cheek. "Look at me! I'm a mess!"

"*You're* a mess?" Maggie waggled her eyebrows. "Compared to me you're ready for a magazine photo-shoot. Before you joined the entertainment at the park, I'd already spent half an hour trying to get the Cat-from-Hell out of the drain. Think I might need to pay a visit to a restroom before joining you for coffee. One look at me and every child in the restaurant will start screaming and running for their mama."

"You don't look *that* bad," said Emily and then really surveyed her friend's disheveled appearance. Maggie had transferred half the mud from the drain onto her hands and then onto her face, probably while wiping off sweat. She frowned. And what was that down the front of Maggie's skirt? Slime? Regurgitated vomit? Or maybe something worse. "Um…on second thoughts…maybe *I'll* order the coffee while *you* go get cleaned up."

Maggie grinned. "Okay. But can you grab me a couple slices of carrot cake with that coffee? I'm starving."

"You're always starving," Emily threw over her shoulder as she headed for the front counter while Maggie went off looking for the restrooms.

After ordering and commandeering a table for two at the back of the room, Emily phoned her mechanic, explaining the crisis with Maggie's car and organizing for it to be towed to the garage, then relaxed in her chair, smiling when Maggie returned ten minutes later looking close to normal. Or as normal as Maggie Post could ever look. What with her fine straight hair that would never sit right, and her complete lack of fashion sense, her best friend was a one off. A one off who always made Emily smile. Look at what she wore today—a calf length floral skirt, damp where she'd been scrubbing at the slime, topped with a rainbow striped shirt—plus her usual laissez-faire attitude that said 'this is the way I am, so if you don't like it, bugger off. It's your loss'.

"Oooh coffee! Thanks, Em, you're a life-saver. If my breath was a bit fresher, I'd kiss you." Maggie dragged out a chair and collapsed into it with the decorum of a teenager instead of a woman in the twilight of her thirties. She took a gulp of her cappuccino and closed her eyes, her face reflecting absolute bliss the moment the coffee beans hit her taste buds. "Although," she continued placing the cup back on the table and digging her fork into the carrot cake, "you're the last person I expected to be having coffee with on a work day. How come you're not at the clinic doing a blood test on the favorite for the Melbourne Cup or shoveling a tube down the throat of some kid's colicky pony? You're never out and about at this time of day."

It had been a long, trying morning and Emily had no intentions of going into the whys and wherefores of Peter's indiscretions—especially in a public eatery. "Long story involving your brother and his over-active fantasies, but first, let's hear what *you've* been up to. You drop out of circulation for three months, not a phone call, not an email, not even a message via carrier pigeon to let us know where you and that horse-mad daughter of yours disappeared to and today I find you in the park with a battle-scarred cat caught in a drain and demanding to be rescued."

Maggie let out a sigh and her wide shoulders appeared to sag inwards. "Okay, where would you like me to start?"

"Let's start with what the hell you were doing sitting on a bench in a park only a few ks from our clinic?"

"Not intentional. Believe me." Maggie huffed as though she couldn't believe how she'd ended up in the park herself. "Before I could reach the clinic and surprise you and my little brother, the damn car conked out on me. And then, of course, the moment I sat on the park bench, I heard Satan yowling from under the drain."

"Right," said Emily. "And one look at his hissing snarling ugly visage and your heart melted like ice-cream in the sun?"

Maggie quirked one eyebrow but didn't stop chewing on her mouthful of cake. "Well, I couldn't walk away and leave him, could I? You know, Vet's Hypocritical Oath etc."

"And you couldn't find someone *else* to play Superman to your Lois Lane? You had to wait for me to arrive so I could crawl around on the ground with you."

"Always the way, isn't it? Park's crowded when you want a bit of peace and quiet but need help to get down and dirty and every man woman and child disappears." Maggie's eyes twinkled across at her. "Anyway, don't say you didn't enjoy playing in the dirt with me. Just like old times."

Emily returned the grin. It was brilliant having her friend back, drinking coffee, confiding in each other. Yes, it *was* like old times. But the hurt she'd suffered when Maggie left without a word still rankled. "You know, when you took off after Greg's funeral and didn't even let me, your best friend since the cradle, know where you and Judy were hiding out, what was I to think?"

"Sorry, Em. You've a right to be angry." Maggie stopped eating and looked up, a flash of pain darkening her eyes. "It's just that I needed to get away. When I lost Greg it completely threw me and I didn't want to go through the motions with everyone watching and waiting for me to crack. I had to get away from those who knew me, spend my days watching sad movies, crying, eating tubs of chocolate chip ice-cream and only showering when I couldn't stand my own stink any longer."

"And now?"

"Now? I guess I'm almost ready to get on with my life."

"Good," Emily nodded. "So what, you're going back to breeding Australia's best performing thoroughbreds, or look for a job as a vet?"

"Definitely not breeding. Not without Greg. And I don't really want the nightmare hours of a country vet's life again. But somehow, I can't see me working in a suburban clinic either. Maybe it's time I tried something different."

"Ah, well, in that case I might have just the job for you." Emily scrunched her chair closer to the table and leant forward on her elbows. Maybe her friend had reappeared at just the right time. "Maggie, how'd you like to join me in a Mobile Vet consultancy I'm in the process of setting up?"

Maggie opened her mouth to speak, but Emily, noting her friend's familiar eyebrow quirk that clearly said, *hey-I'm-not-a-charity-case*, beat her to it.

"Just listen, okay?" she insisted. "I'm after someone with knowledge of veterinary practices plus breeding, a smattering of business acumen, and an acquaintance with police procedure. And I know Greg always talked his cases through with you."

Maggie chewed on one nail and frowned.

"Come on, Mags, it'd be fun. We could lecture at workshops around Australia, visit race-horse trainers, show-jumping clubs, and occasionally set ourselves up in small country towns for a couple of weeks to provide veterinary services for the locals' animals," Emily said, putting everything into her spiel. Maggie still didn't look convinced. "Hey, we could even help with the round-up after vaccinating cattle on outback cattle stations. You'd love that. And maybe investigate the odd racing scam or two. What do you say, Mags? You'd be a shoo-in for the job."

Maggie carefully laid her cake fork onto the empty plate before reaching across the grey Formica table top to wrap her fingers around one of Emily's hands. "No, you listen to me, Em. Why would you want a partner who'd weigh you down like a bag of old bones? A partner who is still grieving for her husband–"

"Hey, you can grieve while travelling and you'll have me to dump on when life gets overwhelming."

"A partner who hasn't officially worked as a vet for over six years—"

"Poppycock! After giving up veterinary practice to start your horse stud you continued to treat your own horses' injuries at the stud, supervise every new foal's birth and even stitched up your neighbors' cats, dogs, cows, and guinea pigs when they've come banging on your door."

"Who freaks out big time if she has to travel by plane—"

"Enough!" Emily growled. "I want you on board with me because even though your brother is the son of a slimy centipede and has the morals of an alley cat, you, Maggie Post, are my best friend, and I'd trust you with my life."

"But—"

"No more buts." Emily squeezed her friend's fingers. "You've bred champion race horses and worked as a country vet and more importantly, you're a bright intelligent woman who anyone would give their first born to have watching their back in a tough situation. So, why wouldn't I want you as my partner?"

"Okay, okay. I'll think about it." Maggie's smile trembled at the corners of her lips. "But Em, if I *do* decide to join you on your first assignment and can't pull my weight—that's it. I'll be out of your hair faster than you can say: 'what on earth did my brother, Peter, do to you while I was away?'"

Emily dropped Maggie's hand, looked down and brushed a speck of horse drool from the knee of her slacks. Did backstabbing with a rusty blade encapsulate what Peter had done to her? "I don't suppose you have two or three hours to spare?"

"Hey, do Scotsmen wear jockstraps under their kilts when they play cricket?"

Despite her dark mood, Emily laughed at this comeback. Maggie could always do that to her. Shock her out of her crankiness. "I should hope so," she quipped, "or there'd be a lot of uncomfortable Scotsmen walking painfully around those heather-clad moors the day after the match."

"Well, there's my answer/" Maggie countered and drank the last of her coffee in one gulp.

"In that case, let's blow this joint." Emily pushed away from the table and stood up. "I have something special to show you."

"Sounds mysterious."

"It's where I live now. And believe me, when you hear what's been going on in the Harrison household while you and your daughter have been off in the country playing recluse, you might need something stronger than coffee to drink. So, isn't it lucky that as well as a new-fangled coffee machine, I also have a fully stocked bar at home?"

4

The Good Ship 'VETS2U'

Two and a half hours later, Maggie opened her sleep-laden eyes and blinked. Why had Emily parked her Echo on what appeared to be a private wharf beside a river? This wasn't a trickle of a river either. This was the mighty River Murray, and although the word *mighty* wasn't an appropriate term after years of drought, from what she could see, the waterway still appeared healthy enough. Probably due to the enormous amount of water pumped into it from some not-so-lucky town downstream.

While Emily scrambled from the car, arms waving proprietarily toward one of four houseboats tied to the dock by ropes thicker than a well-fed python, Maggie continued to sit and stare through the car window. She watched her friend dancing on the spot like a little kid waiting to open her presents under the Christmas tree.

"This is where I live now, Mags," Emily said and stretched one arm out in the direction of the boat. "Isn't it gorgeous?"

Emily Harrison? Living on a houseboat? The two images in close proximity failed to compute in Maggie's tired brain. "But, Em," she said. "You get seasick."

Emily tutted. "In case you didn't notice, Mags, this is a river—not the sea."

'But it's still a boat," Maggie persisted and shook her head.

"But this boat is tied to the wharf." Emily enunciated each word slowly as if to a five-year old. "It's a *house* boat." She bent down and poked her head through the open car window and frowned at Maggie. "Now, get your booty out here, pronto. 'Cos I want to show you what I've done with the interior decoration." Her face lit up like a Christmas star. "I guess you'd call it sort of maritime, with a touch of country cottage."

"Okay, okay. Geez, Em, you're full of surprises today." Maggie maneuvered her large frame from the car then slowly straightened in an attempt to remove the kinks and knots caused by travelling hunched asleep in the passenger seat of Emily's Echo. She knew the vet-clinic owned a large four-wheel drive, so Maggie could never work out why her friend had a penchant for small cars for her personal use. Okay, they might be perfect for petite women and pointy-eared elves but they weren't designed for people like Maggie Post whose long legs and well-padded curves tended to get stuck inside. Give her a decent sized Ford or a Holden station-wagon any day.

Momentarily distracted by the roar of an engine that almost wiped out the strident screams of the white sulphur-crested cockatoos busy stripping bark from a nearby red gum, Maggie blinked again. Then let out a sigh as two young bronzed twenty-somethings, dressed in nothing but board shorts, flashed by on the river, one languidly working the controls of a motor boat while the other yahooed his adrenalin-fired prowess on water skis behind.

Made Maggie feel every one of her thirty-eight years.

"Hmm…not bad eye candy," said Emily with a wink. "All adds to the magnificent scenery around here. Now, if you're quite ready, let's go inside."

With a shake of her head, Maggie took a step closer to the houseboat. She peered at the pink front door, the rhythmic movement of the lower deck and the numerous portholes lined up on each side of the hull, or whatever one called the sides of a boat. The reality of Emily owning a houseboat still didn't make sense. Was her friend going through early menopause? Or had she been invaded by the character of river-loving

Ratty while reading Kenneth Grahame's *The Wind in the Willows*? And where the heck did her brother, Emily's husband, Peter, fit into all this?

Admittedly her mind was foggy due to getting out of bed at dawn and driving the 100ks to Burra and then another hour and a half on to Nuriootpa this morning, but she could swear Emily hadn't mentioned the word 'houseboat' on the trip here.

Or had she?

She remembered crossing the River Murray by punt at one stage of the journey but hadn't woken up again until they were driving through the Riverland town of Barmera. And of course when they left the main road and drove along a track running parallel with the river, she'd dropped off to sleep again. In fact, it wasn't until the car pulled up on this sparse sunburnt patch of grass separating the dirty brown river from a large rambling house with at least eight chimneys and ivy crawling up its walls and a paddock with a couple of horses grazing at the far end, that she actually woke up and took in her surroundings.

Which of course brought her back to Emily's houseboat.

Unable to put the inspection off any longer, she hitched up her skirt and followed Emily through the garish pink door and down three wooden steps. Wow! She stopped to survey the scene in front of her. Warm colors predominated below deck and the living area was much larger than she'd imagined. As she followed Emily through the boat, Maggie took in soft squishy sofas, a tiny galley with the most gorgeous eating area that looked out onto the river through a wall length glass sliding door, a couple of bedrooms—or she guessed you'd call them cabins—a large flat screen television set into the wall in front of the sofas and a built-in workstation with a desktop computer, printer, file cupboards and bookshelves behind the sofas.

No wonder Emily had fallen in love with her new home. What was there not to love?

"It's beautiful, Em. You've done a fabulous job of making the boat a home away from home." Her eyes settled on the temptation of the sitting area. "And that sofa looks soft and squishy enough to drop into and spend the rest of my life sleeping and watching television."

"Still prefer white?" Emily selected a bottle of wine from an inbuilt bar and held it up for her friend's scrutiny.

"Oooh yes, please," With a sigh of pleasure Maggie flopped onto the sofa and closed her eyes. This was absolute bliss.

"No time for sleeping, Maggie. We have things to discuss." Emily waved the bottle of Chardonnay in Maggie's direction with one hand while snaffling two glasses from a cupboard with the other.

'We do?'

"We do." Emily filled both glasses with wine and handed one to Maggie. "Now, you were telling me what you thought of my boat."

Maggie laughed. "The boat's gorgeous. I love it." She cradled the glass in both hands and raised one eyebrow. "Do you have plans to ever take it out on the river?"

"Have no idea how to handle a boat. At the moment, the only time this baby gets moved is once a fortnight, when Sam, the odd-job guy, comes and takes it to the nearest marina to empty the bilge and the waste." She took a sip of her full-bodied Shiraz. "At a prearranged time of course."

"What happens when there's a storm and the river gets rough?"

Emily glanced up and grinned. "Rivers don't get rough, Mags, and anyway I could always book into a hotel for the night."

"Or seek refuge in that old ivy-covered house by the dock. Who lives up there? Some forgotten rock-star—or The Ghost of Christmas Past?"

Emily strolled across to the bookcase and picked out a gaudy paperback. "Never met the guy, but the real-estate agent said an author by the name of Edward G. Peters owns the house and the wharf." She held the book up for Maggie to see: *Blood and Gore* by Edward G. Peters. "You want to read it some time. There's enough spine-chilling creepiness in this book to keep your bedroom light burning all night."

Maggie rolled her eyes. "In that case I think I'll give it a miss, thank you."

"Edward G is a bit of a hermit so I pay rent for the berth through an agent." Emily slipped the book back onto the shelf. "Anyway, enough of the mysterious author, what I want to know is what have you done with that bubbly horse-mad daughter of yours? Traded her in for a normal, standard model?"

Maggie laughed. Emily, without children of her own, doted on her niece. In fact, Maggie had to continually step in and prevent Emily from spoiling her rotten. "No, I enrolled Judy at Trinity College a couple of months ago. It's a boarding school where the kids bring their own horse and the school counts Equestrian as a subject on their curriculum."

"Judy took Alex to school with her?" Emily sounded skeptical as she topped up Maggie's glass. "And she'll be riding him every day?"

Maggie nodded.

"You'll never get the kid to come home for the holidays."

"First I have to buy a house for her to come home to. When you found me in the park I was on my way to your clinic to see if I could stay with you and Peter for a few weeks. Just until I find somewhere to live."

"Why not stay here with me?"

"But what about when Judy comes home for the holidays?"

"What about it?" said Emily and shrugged. "Hey, if I know Judy, she'll love the idea of living on a boat. She can bunk in with you. And there's a paddock nearby for Alex." Emily grinned. "Anyway, if you and I are going to work together…"

Maggie shook her head. "I haven't said I'd take the job yet, Em. I said I'd *think* about it." She took a sip of her wine. Cool and fresh as it slid down her throat. "And while I'm thinking about this job offer—you can tell me what my brainless brother's been up to."

"Brainless is too kind a word to describe him."

"What on earth did he do to induce you to leave your huge suburban house with all its mod cons to live in a houseboat on the river?" Maggie frowned as she watched Emily refill her glass, set it on the side table and then drop onto the sofa beside her, shoulders slumped. This was worse than she thought.

Emily reached for a tissue, blew her nose and tossed it in the bin. She grabbed a second tissue from the box and let out a sigh that tore at Maggie's heart. "Peter's been cheating on me."

"Oh, no, Em! I'm so sorry." Maggie wrapped both arms around her friend and hugged her, not letting go until she felt the rigidity leave Emily's shoulders. "I didn't think even *he* could be as stupid as that."

"I'm the stupid one, Mags. I should have realized he was playing around." Emily's fingers plucked at the tissue, shredding it into tiny pieces. "All the clichéd cheating husband symptoms were there in full 3D color for me to see. You know, the faint smell of a perfume I'd never wear in a million years, the phone calls where no-one answers and then the caller hangs up, the packet of condoms I found in his lab-coat pocket, working back late at the surgery for an emergency call with no sign of the 'emergency' in the hospital stables the following morning." She shook her head as though she still couldn't believe the story herself. "But whenever I challenged Peter, he always came up with a convincing excuse. Even made me feel like I was a nagging wife and accused me of being paranoid."

"I'd like to know how he explained the packet of condoms in his coat pocket, when you're on the pill."

"Said he bought them for young Steve Watts, the lad who picks up and delivers our blood samples to the Lab. Said Steve was too shy to go to the chemist and ask for condoms, so Peter volunteered. Just hadn't got around to giving them to him yet."

"Riiiight. And the perfume?"

"Oh, Peter had an answer for that one too. He said our receptionist, who I later discovered had it off with him in one of the empty stables, was dabbing perfume on her wrists after a messy operation and the horse started coming to, nudged her arm with his head and knocked the perfume bottle over. Of course a few drops conveniently splashed onto the collar of Peter's shirt."

"Of course." Maggie ground her teeth together. "Peter was always good at making up outlandish stories when he was a kid. Dad and Mum figured he'd become a writer when he grew up—or a politician."

"I guess I just didn't want to accept the truth, Mags. That is, until I found his collection of trophy panties hidden in the bottom of his wardrobe…"

Emily's voice trailed off into silence, broken eventually by the ringing of the phone. While Emily reached for the phone and began talking, Maggie carried her drink out onto the deck, sliding the glass door shut behind her.

She should take a stick to her boneheaded brother. Knock some sense into him. Why couldn't he see that quick flashes of passion performed against a stable wall or on the operating table lasted minutes, whereas when he married Emily she'd promised to love him forever? And now…he'd blown it. Big time.

Breathing in the cool river air, she leant over the rail and surveyed the creepy old mansion belonging to the writer guy. Surely, what was his name—Edward G Peters—didn't live there on his own. One old guy rattling around in an eight-roomed house didn't make sense. Although a house of that age probably had its own resident ghost or three to keep him company. And she guessed he had a housekeeper come in each day to clean and cook his meals. Writers usually lost track of time and forgot to eat if someone didn't cook for them. Or so she'd heard.

The two horses she'd seen grazing on the far side of the paddock beside the house had wandered closer. They appeared to be thoroughbreds. In fact, on closer inspection, the horses looked very familiar…

Inside the boat, Maggie heard Emily hang up the phone. She turned to greet her friend as the glass door opened and she stepped outside. "Emily Harrison," Maggie said, her voice reedy, ready to crack. "What are Pride and Prejudice doing in the writer guy's paddock?"

"Ah, so you spotted them." Emily patted Maggie's shoulder. "When you disappeared and all your horses were auctioned off, I couldn't let your two favorites go, now could I? So, I bought them, knowing you'd want them back once you came to your senses. Meanwhile, they're paddocked over there until you're ready for them."

Maggie felt hot tears roll down her cheek. After the funeral, when she was out of her mind with grief, not thinking straight and only wanting to get away and cry, her friend, Emily, knowing she'd regret selling her two beloved horses, Pride and Prejudice, had gone to the auction and bought them for her.

"How can I ever thank you, Em?"

"Don't worry, I'll think of something." Emily's grin spread outwards from the corners of her mouth. "And now, guess what? That phone-call was from the Chief Steward/racing manager of a new bush racetrack opening in a week's time. Mags, we've landed our first assignment."

"We?"

"Of course."

Maggie grinned. "I don't deserve a friend like you."

"I agree, you don't," said Emily, giving Maggie a push.

Maggie laughed and pushed her back.

"So…now that's all sorted," said Emily lifting her glass to clink with Maggie's. "Just think, next week, we'll be giving lectures and officiating at the opening of a little bush track in a country town fifty kilometers on from Port Augusta. Just a tiny dot on the map, called Kangaroo Downs."

5

Kangaroo Downs here we Come

"Hurry up. We're leaving in ten minutes, Mags."

Maggie squeezed her suitcase into the hatch of Emily's elf-sized car and frowned. If she joined her petite friend in this *Vets2U* business, the first thing they'd do was buy a decent sized car for transport. Preferably a van. A van with lots of leg room, comfortable seats, and top-of-the-range air-con. A van with a large open space at the rear to house a portable refrigerator for their vaccinations and other injectables and plenty of cupboards for their veterinary equipment and various medications needed to treat local injured animals wherever they traveled.

With a grunt Maggie shoved at the offending suitcase with both hands resulting in it moving a couple of hairs breadths further into the hatch-back. Oh, God. How was she going to stay sane, jammed into the Elf-Mobile all the way to Kangaroo Downs? It was a six hour drive. And they couldn't even use her old Ford station wagon because she'd cooked the motor driving so far without water—or so Emily's mechanic had informed her while rolling his eyes skywards.

"I'm just going to slip down to the paddock and say goodbye to the horses," Maggie called back, trying unsuccessfully to shut the boot of the car.

"We're scheduled to meet Craig Benham at Kangaroo Down's track at three o'clock, so don't fuss with those fur-babies for too long."

"Okay, boss-lady." Maggie gave the reluctant case one last gargantuan heave, slammed the hatch shut and then headed for the paddock.

She could see Pride and Prejudice grazing at the far end, so close together they were almost touching. As she opened the gate, then latched it behind her, she let out her special whistle. The whistle they knew so well. Both horses lifted their heads, nostrils wide, ears alert. And then, while she cut the binder twine and scattered a bale of lucerne hay on the ground to add to the large round bale of oaten hay in their paddock, Pride, a gelding with the most exquisite head and body and a race record to match, galloped up to her, snorting and whinnying his delight at her visit. Prejudice trotted up behind him and tucked her head under Maggie's arm, almost begging her not to leave them again.

"I'm sorry, guys," she said tickling Prejudice behind the ears. "I'll only be gone for a few days."

Pride danced around her, snuffling and blowing hot air in her face. She stretched up and wrapped one arm around his shiny bay neck, tears threatening to roll down her cheeks. How could she have been so grief-stricken after Greg's funeral that she'd ordered the auctioneer to not only sell her property, but to sell all her horses? A mistake she'd spend the rest of her life regretting. It was bad enough she'd lost all her brood mares and their foals but if Emily hadn't come to the rescue, she'd have lost Pride and Prejudice as well.

She hugged both horses, accepting Prejudice's own personal gesture of love, a messy sneeze which meant she'd need to go back to her cabin and change her shirt. Then, after making sure the paddock gate was firmly latched behind her, Maggie left the horses happily munching on hay and made her way back to the houseboat.

She lifted her chin. It was time to suck up her grief and help make Emily's new company, *Vets2U*, make a go of it. Even if it meant driving all the way to Kangaroo Down in Emily's damn Elf-mobile.

*****

"And do you know what *else* that money grabbing weasel of a brother-of-yours asked for?"

Beside her, Emily's voice slid up another decibel, causing Maggie to seriously contemplate taking her hands off the steering wheel and putting her fingers in both ears.

They'd been traveling for what felt like days but was probably only five hours. The sameness and the heat and the confines of their claustrophobic vehicle were starting to get to her. She'd read in this morning's paper, today was the fifth day in a row that the temperature expected to reach 40 degrees. Seemed like the weather forecaster was spot on.

Seemingly oblivious to Maggie's discomfort and lack of answers, Emily continued her tirade. "That slimy six-legged maggot wants my house! Can you believe it? That-that *Don Juan* wants to take my house away from me!"

Maggie sighed, blinked at the never-ending road in front of them and forced herself to answer. She couldn't win. Her asinine brother was the offender and her friend, Emily, the victim, while *she* was the meat in the sandwich. "Come on, Em," she soothed, "you don't *need* the house. You have a gorgeous houseboat to live in now—and just think— Peter will have to go into debt to pay you out. He'll be paying for his indiscretions for a long, long time."

"That's not the point. *He's* the guilty party here. What if he brings one of his-his 'conquests' into our house? Into our *bed*?"

Maggie took one hand off the wheel, reached over and squeezed her friend's hand. She didn't bother agreeing or disagreeing. Nothing she could say would penetrate the thick wall of hurt Emily was experiencing. Best to let her friend rave on until she ran out of steam. Curse until she cleared the latest phone call from Peter's lawyer from her system.

Instead, Maggie focused on the sight of a nicely set-up racing stable, *Kangaroo Lodge*, coming up on her right. Since leaving Port Augusta they'd passed a few racing stables, seemingly in the middle of nowhere, from barbed-wire-fenced dirt paddocks with three-corner shelters for the dust-encrusted horses, to professionally built brick stable blocks with irrigated paddocks and shiny, contented horses standing under trees, flicking their tails at the persistent flies.

The establishment they were passing now, *Kangaroo Lodge*, covered close to fifty acres, sported its own trial track and even boasted a circular horse-pool, where a young girl about 16, dressed in shorts, tank top and large straw hat walked around the circumference of the pool holding a lead-rope in one hand and a book in the other, while her equine charge, a bright bay horse stretching his neck and head skywards, swam his required laps for the day.

"Look at that! Bet *they* breed and train a few winners."

"Love the girl reading a book," said Emily taking a deep breath and letting it out slowly. "Looks like swimming the horses is a chore she's stuck with every day."

"And why not finish your latest paperback at the same time?"

"Exactly." Emily shrugged her shoulders and stretched. "How much further to Kangaroo Downs?"

"Not far. We should be coming to a truck-stop diner in about ten minutes and then it's only a kilometer further on to Kangaroo Downs. I'll have to stop at the diner though."

"Why?"

"Otherwise I'll have to stop the car now and dive behind one of those scrawny looking bushes growing on the side of the road."

"That desperate, hey?"

"You'd better believe it."

Suddenly Maggie' stomach rumbled like a volcano threatening to erupt, diverting her thoughts of being caught in an uncompromising position by the occupants of the next passing car. "*And* I'm hungry enough to eat a live cow."

Emily shook her head. "You're totally disgusting, Mags. If you'd been around in the cave man era, while everyone else ran screaming away from an approaching dinosaur, you'd be hiding behind a bush waiting with your club and your stone knife and fork at the ready."

"Dinosaurs were extinct when cave men were around."

"So they say, but how many cave men have you associated with who could verify that theory?"

Maggie cocked her head to one side. "Well, let's see. There's Greg's old boss, toad-faced Detective Sergeant Trevor Tucker. He has the mentality of a cave man—wives should be tied to the kitchen stove and not in the work-force."

"And what about Jacob Bean, that hot looking salesman from *Acute* who flogs equine products to vet clinics?" Emily whistled and rolled her eyes. "He'd look great in nothing but a minimal furry loin cloth and a—"

"Enough!" Maggie groaned. "That image is burning the insides of my eyelids."

Signs of civilization started to appear on the side of the road. First a faded poster advertising Kangaroo Downs' local pub and depicting a guy in jeans, navy singlet and an Akubra hat, drinking a can of VB, followed by another sign telling them, *Joe and Jean's Truck-stop Diner serves delicious truck-sized meals.*

"Yay!" said Maggie. "While I attend to business, can you order sausages, onions, bacon, eggs and chips for me?"

"A truck-sized meal?"

"You bet. And I'll eat every morsel."

A minute later Maggie screeched to a stop between two monster trucks parked outside the diner, and almost yanked the car door off its hinges before sprinting in the direction of a battle scarred wooden door.

A door with a generic figure in a dress painted on the front.

*****

Maggie wrinkled her nose. A smell, sweet and sickly and sort of familiar hung thick in the air. Familiar, but she couldn't quite put her finger on it. Geez Louise! You'd think splashing around a smidgeon of disinfectant and squirting a modicum of air freshener in each stall would come under Basic Health Essentials 101, wouldn't you?

However, this was not the time to worry about the cleanliness of Jack and Jean's Truck-stop restrooms. Taking a deep breath, Maggie uncrossed her legs and shuffled forward. She had more important things to attend to.

The first stall displayed an engaged sign so Maggie pushed against the door of stall number two and hurried inside.

As she sat down, her mobile played the theme song from *The Titanic*. Maggie reached across and dragged her bag closer, dug inside and as she grabbed her phone, her lipstick fell from her bag and rolled under the cubicle wall and into the stall next door. Damn. That was her favorite lipstick. Rose of Orleans. And she'd spent half an hour hunting for exactly that shade at the Mall the day before.

Cursing under her breath, Maggie finished her ablutions, plonked herself back on the toilet seat and answered the phone. It was her daughter, Judy. "Darling, if it's not life-threatening, I'm in a bit of a bind at the moment, so can I ring you back?" she said. Evidently it wasn't life-threatening, only the biggest news of the week, according to her horse-mad, daughter. Alex had negotiated a clear course of four foot jumps that morning and her instructor had singled her out for praise. "That's amazing. I'm so proud of you and Alex. Look, I'll ring you later and we'll have a long talk and you can tell me about every jump on the course. Okay?"

Ending the call, Maggie shoved the phone back into her bag and sighed. Now to rescue her lipstick.

When she'd dashed into the restroom a few minutes earlier there'd been an engaged signal showing on the door of the next cubicle. She hadn't heard the door open or a tap running, so the occupant must still be in there. Maybe, if she asked very sweetly, the woman might return her lipstick.

"Um…hello," she called out, grimacing at her red-faced predicament. "I don't suppose you could slip my lipstick back underneath, could you? It's my favorite color."

No answer.

"If you just give it a little push, I can do the rest," she added, still hopeful. This was so embarrassing.

Nothing…

Not even a shuffle or a cough from the adjoining stall.

In fact, she hadn't heard any movement since she'd arrived. Perhaps whoever was in there had fainted in the heat. Must be close to 45 degrees under this god-awful tin roof.

"Hey, are you okay? Do you need any help?"

While squatting on the seat, Maggie folded in the middle and bent over until her head touched the ground. Although causing slight dizziness, the maneuver worked. She could now see into the next cubicle. Who'd have thought all those yoga exercises she'd paid for over the years would come in handy one day? Of course she only had a limited view…but was that a pair of men's black shoes only inches away from her lipstick? Too far away for her to reach. And when she twisted her neck to catch a higher view—was that a pair of men's gray trousers with a knife-edged crease running up the front?

Huh?

Maggie bolted upright. There was either a cross dressing female in the next stall or a man who'd misinterpreted the figure-in-a-dress painted on the restroom door.

Or was the man occupying the next stall more sinister? Like a rapist sitting in wait for his next victim.

Maggie squatted more squarely on the plastic rim and rested her elbows on her knees. Before taking action, she needed to weigh up every one of her options.

Make a run for it?

Doubtful. She'd never won a race in her life. Not even the egg and spoon race she'd joined in with the under 10's at the last Sunday school picnic.

Confront him?

Well, that depended on the man's size. Bit hard to judge when all she had to go on were his shiny shoes and the bottom third of his trousers. Maybe she could climb up on the seat, sneak an investigative peep over the top of the stall and check out the opposition? That way she could ascertain whether or not she could take the guy out if necessary. Okay, her only weapon was her trusty tote bag, but hey, at that same Sunday school picnic, she'd fronted up to an aggressive kangaroo with her tote-bag and chased it away from a trestle table full of tomato and lettuce sandwiches.

But that was three months, countless containers of choc-chip ice cream, and ten kilos ago.

So what? She had now moved on. Determined, Maggie smoothed down her skirt and pinched the close-fitting top away from her sweaty armpits, hefted her ninety-five kilos up onto the seat and eased her head over the top of the partition.

She blinked. Confused. A man sat on the toilet. He was fully clothed. There was a buzzing of flies around his head. And a stillness that struck her as unnatural.

Was he asleep?

"Hey, you in there, can't you read? This is the ladies restroom."

When the man failed to acknowledge her, she stood on tiptoe to get a better view. And that's when she noticed the man's neck was positioned at a very strange angle. The familiar sickly sweet smell came from him. And when she looked closer, there was a large jagged hole in his head.

Maggie closed her eyes.

She felt sick.

She lurched off the seat, leaned over the bowl and then, after a couple of dry heaves, began unloading the recently consumed coffee and crisps, plus her breakfast of toast and four Weetabix, and even the tuna salad with garlic sauce and squeezed lemon she'd eaten for dinner the night before.

6

Restroom Surprise

Emily slid from the car and stood up. She swayed a little as one high heel stuck in the uneven ground and made a grab for the car door to steady herself. Maybe she should have worn something other than a low-necked chemise, skin tight Chloe jeans, and killer Dior stiletto-heeled boots to venture into the Australian bush. And then she shrugged. Working with animals saw her always dressed in serviceable overalls and sturdy boots, her hair tousled and either mud or something worse smudged on her face, so she loved dressing up when she was off duty.

Away from the car's air-conditioning, the heat slammed into her like a live force field. It snatched at her breath and made her blink. Probably sizzle past 40 degrees before the day was over. And here she was caught without sunscreen and a hat—both packed in the bowels of her suitcase in the boot of her car.

She eased her silky grey chemise away from her damp skin and licked her dry lips. God she was thirsty. And hungry. An icy cold bottle of Evian water and a salad sandwich would really hit the spot.

Mincing towards the diner, she noticed two working dogs, one a kelpie, the other an Australian cattle dog, both tied to a tree out front. A scrawny tree with little to no shade. Talking softly to the dogs she bent to feel the water in their bowl. Warm. She frowned. Probably working sheep dogs or maybe guard dogs, but all the lackluster creatures were chasing or guarding today was shade under a bare tree. If they belonged to the proprietor of the diner, why weren't they in suitable kennels around the back? She made a mental note to give both *Joe and Jean* a full-on serve. No animal should be left to fend for itself in 40 degree heat.

She glanced around her. Judging by the large number of monster sized trucks parked out front, she guessed most of the paying customers were truck drivers with appetites to match their vehicles. Which led her to the cooking smells emanating from inside the diner.

Sausages. Onions. Bacon. Eggs. Chips.

Maybe she'd been hasty, scoffing at Maggie's choice of meal. She let the tantalizing aroma wash over her, infiltrate her senses, tickle her taste buds and let out a sigh which sounded more like a moan. Then, keen to get in out of the scorching sun, Emily scaled the three wooden steps leading up to the front door of the diner. At the top of the steps she stopped, wiped the sweat from her eyes and glanced beside her into an adjoining one-acre paddock, the ground mostly dirt, which was par for this time of year. She was pleased to see a huge shady gum tree growing in the middle of the paddock and a dusty green shade-cloth awning attached to stables nearby. Looked like the guy cared more for his horses than he did for his dogs.

A goat, mostly black with white patches, ears at half-mast, tangled beard half white, half black, stared unblinkingly at her from over the fence. When she put her hand on the front door intending to launch herself into the diner, the goat let out a plaintive baa and then stood on its hind legs and attempted to climb over the fence.

What the…?

Near the goat stood a large raw-boned chestnut gelding, while a second horse, a smaller, dark bay with a black mane and tail, slouched at the back of the paddock, half-in, half-out of a stable. The chestnut, his warm chocolatey-colored eyes centered on his friend the goat's gymnastics, tipped his head to one side. His bottom lip protruded and his tail swished rhythmically from side to side—a horse's way of disturbing the constant biting of the ever-present summer flies.

Emily turned around slowly. The frantic goat, his round marble eyes pinned on her, once again pushed off the ground with both hind legs, this time almost succeeding in scrambling over the fence.

Was the bearded one trying to tell her something?

"What's up Goat?" she asked and walked back down the steps to remove the goat's front legs from the top rail. He shook his head and butted her hand away, but now he had her attention, seemed happy to settle back down four-on-the-floor.

Emily leant over the fence to check the water trough. Full to the brim—so it wasn't water he was after. She scanned the paddock, but there didn't seem to be any loose dogs or other predators around.

"I think you're having me on, Goat." She leant forward to scratch him on the top of the head between his two stubby horns. "Great trick, but sorry, it's too hot to stand outside and play games with... "And that's when she noticed the yellow bucket. The small yellow bucket which the big chestnut horse had stuck one of his front hooves inside and evidently couldn't get it out again.

"Damn!" She looked around. Not a soul in sight. All inside filling their stomachs with bacon, eggs, onions and chips. And where the heck was Maggie? She should be finished in the restrooms by now. "You goofy horse!" she told the big chestnut who smiled at her with droopy lips. "Can't you see I'm not dressed for doing good deeds? This swanky top cost me over a hundred dollars and how on earth do you expect me to come into the paddock in *these* shoes?"

The horse's droopy lips drooped even further and he stamped his bucket-clad foot to remove an extended family of flies from his legs.

Emily glanced over her shoulder again but no Maggie in sight. So, with a resigned sigh she bent down and carefully plucked off the killer Dior stiletto-heeled black boots which she'd bought, against her better judgement, the day after she'd found Greg's stash of panties, lined the boots up neatly on the bottom step leading to the diner and climbed through the fence.

This shouldn't take long.

A shiny green halter with an iridescent pink lead rope had been tossed on the ground beside the water trough so Emily scooped it up and carefully picked her way on bare feet across to the horse. "Only a dumbass would get his foot stuck in a bucket!" she told him. "But if you want me to help, you'll have to put your head down. The air's more horse-friendly down here and even on tip-toe I can't reach to put the halter on up there." Geez, this horse had to be close to 18hh. Enormous for a thoroughbred.

With what passed for a smile, or gas, the horse flopped his bottom lip up and down as he nuzzled her, transferring green slime to her hundred-dollar top. She sighed and shook her head, then slipped the halter over his nose and did up the buckle around his ears. She couldn't help grinning at the big lug. He really was quite sweet. And if she didn't remove the bucket from his foot he could take a scare, gallop round the paddock and hurt himself.

Emily led the horse toward a tie-up rail over near the water trough and as he walked beside her she could hear the soft thud of three hooves and then a clunk for the fourth.

"Don't worry, I'll have you out of that bucket in a jiffy." Emily tied the horse up and dodged the inquisitive goat, who now he'd succeeded in gaining her attention, was quite happy to assist her in her effort to remove the bucket. She bent down and lifted the horse's right front leg off the ground to examine the problem more closely.

By now the dark bay, attracted to the drama acting out at the front of the paddock had wandered across to snuffle in Emily's hair. Not to be outdone, the patient bent his head down and slobbered on her expensive chemise. Again. "Come on, guys," she said, batting their heads away gently. "Give me a bit of room to work here."

She gripped the sides of the bucket and tugged but it was jammed tightly around the horse's hoof. "Damn," she said. "Looks like I'll have to cut it off."

She stood up, stretched the kinks from her back and moved across to rescue her shoulder bag from Goat's mouth. Before entering the paddock she'd hung the bag on the fence but of course that hadn't stopped Goat from grabbing it. "Should be a pair of nail scissors in here," she told him and burrowed around inside until she found the scissors, then dropped the bag over the other side of the fence out of the goat's reach.

"Won't be long now." Emily ran a hand along the chestnut's sleek, well-muscled neck, then bent to take a closer look at the problem bucket.

"Right. Here we go." As she sawed away at the obstacle, she realized that although the nail-scissors were tiny, the plastic bucket was old and weathered. It was like sawing through steak with a butter knife. Slow, but manageable.

At last she felt the bucket loosen around the wedged hoof. "Hey," she informed the animal-gathering. "I think we have lift-off!"

With one final tug, the bucket dropped off the horse's leg. "There," she said. "Now, any chance you lot can stay out of trouble for five minutes while I go get something to eat?"

As Emily slipped the horse's halter off and walked across to hang it on the fence, she heard a high-pitched scream. It was Maggie. And she was bolting out of the restrooms like the entire cast of The Walking Dead were chasing her.

"What happened?" she asked as Maggie, face pale, gasping for breath, reached the paddock and sagged against the fence. "You look like you've seen a ghost."

"It's worse! There's a dead guy in the restrooms. And he's been murdered."

"Whaat?"

"Part of his face has been blown away."

Emily blinked at her friend. Had she bumped her head on the cubicle door on the way in?

"Oh, Em, it was horrible." Maggie swayed and her hands tightened on the fence as though to stop herself from falling. "The blood. And the flies… they're buzzing all around him." Maggie's voice cracked. "Can you ring the police, Em? My hands are shaking so much I'd drop my phone."

Emily slipped under the fence and put an arm around her friend. She could feel Maggie's heart thumping as though trying to escape her body and run away. This was real. She *had* seen a dead body. "Okay, okay," she said and gave Maggie a squeeze. "But I'd better go take a look myself, first.

"No, Em—"

"Won't take a minute. I'll just have a quick peep so I can fill the police in on what's happened when I ring them." Without waiting for an answer, Emily hooked arms with her shaking friend. "Think you can show me where he is?"

"But what if the murderer is still around?"

Hmm…Maggie's last comment made sense. What if the murderer *was* still around? Emily peered closely at the thick bushes growing nearby. Maybe she should take Maggie's word for it and just ring the police then hide inside the diner out of danger.

"No!" She straightened her shoulders and marched toward the restrooms, dragging a reluctant Maggie behind her. How could she ring the police about a dead body when she hadn't even seen it? Maybe Maggie had made a mistake and the guy was merely a drunk who'd wandered into the wrong restroom, and passed out…

Two minutes later, Emily, with Maggie in tow, exploded through the door marked with a generic figure dressed in a skirt, and made a mad dash for the entrance to *Joe and Jean's Diner*. Nope. The man sitting on the toilet was *not* a drunk. It had taken less than thirty seconds for the persistent flies, and the fact that he only had half a face, to convince Emily of that.

And even though she paused to scoop up her Dior, stiletto-heeled, black boots from the bottom step leading to the diner, Emily was still two strides ahead of Maggie by the time they burst through the glass doors and launched themselves inside.

"Who's the proprietor of this establishment?" Emily shouted at the two startled people serving behind the order-counter. "'Cos I have a serious complaint to make about your restrooms."

7

Retreat or Stay

Maggie had never seen a group of big burly men move quite so quickly.

After Emily imparted the news of finding a murdered man in Jean and Joe's restrooms in a voice loud enough to be heard in the next state, the diner erupted like the fourth of July.

One minute the place was alive with truck-drivers, talking, laughing, and enjoying their meal—the next, the diner was empty.

While Emily rang and filled in the gruesome details to the police, Maggie slumped on a stool by the window. She blinked at the farcical scenes being staged in the parking lot outside. Truck doors banged. Men shouted at each other. Headlights flicked on and off. Musical horns pierced the air as trucks geared from the parking lot, drivers intent on getting as far from the crime scene as possible before the police arrived.

"My God," said Emily as she grabbed a bottle of Evian water from the refrigerator. "They left in a hurry."

Maggie surveyed the diner and shook her head. Half eaten sausages, slices of bacon piled high with ketchup and still-steaming coffee were the only signs that truckers preferred keeping to their schedule over sustenance. "One way to clear a room, I guess."

"And what about us? Are we going to hightail it out of here and leave the owners of the diner to talk to the police when they arrive?"

If only! Maggie sighed. "Unfortunately, I was the one who discovered the body so I have to stick around."

"Mmm…guess so." Emily sat down beside her. "I still can't get the image of that poor man out of my head."

Maggie shook her head. "Me either."

Joe, the proprietor of the diner, a tea towel tucked into the waist of his jeans and dark oily hair straggling onto the collar of his cowboy shirt, lifted the hinged section of the counter and strode into the dining area.

"The cops rang back. They'll be here in about ten minutes." He scowled at Maggie and Emily, his eyes ripping into them as though *they* were the cause of his now empty diner. "Are you sure you two haven't been smoking funny bacca?" he asked them. "Can't see how I wouldn't notice a dead body in my own restrooms. It's not like I don't check them every day."

"But do you actually *open* the cubicle doors and go inside to clean the toilets?" Maggie narrowed her eyes at him. The health department would be stretching to give this man's facilities a D minus. And if she hadn't found the dead guy sitting on the toilet, he'd probably still be sitting there in a weeks' time.

"Don't take our word for it—check the body out for yourself," suggested Emily.

"Hang on," said Maggie jumping up and sending Emily a frown. "You can't just let anyone—a potential suspect—enter a crime scene."

"A potential suspect? What do you mean?" Joe's voice rose then cracked, his eyes bugged and spittle flew from his thick lips as he pushed his face into hers. Dodging garlic breath and flying saliva, Maggie backed away until her thigh hit the table. Geez, this guy was as volatile as a live grenade.

"In that case, why don't you go with him, Mags?" Completely ignoring the big man's red face and clenched fists, Emily turned to Joe. "My friend's husband was a policeman. She knows a lot about procedure."

Maggie shook her head. Okay, maybe she *did* know a lot about procedure—after all, Greg had been a stickler for procedure while in the force and spoke about it constantly at home. Another sigh slammed into her heart. But no amount of procedure was able to help him in that last drug bust that left him lying in a pool of blood, his life ebbing away with every breath.

"Sorry, Em," she said, struggling to keep the quiver from her voice, "but if Joe is determined to check out the body before the police arrive, he can either go by himself, or you can accompany him. I need a drink." She stumbled towards the large refrigerator, pulled out a bottle of orange juice and waved the bottle at them. "But whatever you do, don't touch anything. It's a crime scene. Actually the entire restroom and the area in front are part of the crime scene. There could be clues almost anywhere. A button that went flying. Something that fell out of the victim or the perpetrator's pocket and rolled under the wall into the next stall. Anything. Why not wait until the police arrive?"

"I need to make sure there *is* a body out there," said Joe. "If the police arrive and it's all a hoax I'll look a right fool."

"Okay. Okay. But it's on your head." She held up both hands, palms outwards in a sign of supplication. "But if you must disturb a crime scene—do what I did—climb onto the seat in the cubicle next door and look over the top."

Emily pushed herself away from the counter ready to follow the still-scowling Joe from the diner. "By the way," she said when she'd caught up to him and tugged on his shirtsleeve. "Do those two dogs out the front belong to you?"

Joe flicked his scowl in her direction and grunted while Maggie rolled her eyes. Her friend always picked the worst times to lecture people. And as for Joe, was he normally this rude and angry, or just worried about the murdered man being discovered on his premises?

"Thought so," said Emily and marched to the fridge, grabbed two bottles of spring water from the display and handed both bottles to Joe.

"I don't want these," he said.

"Maybe not, but your dogs do. One bottle is to replace the warm water in their dish and the other to pour over the dogs to cool them down."

"You're joking!"

Maggie couldn't suppress her grin. "Emily *never* jokes about cruelty to animals."

"But-but I'm not wasting expensive spring water on dogs. Spring water costs money."

"It's either that or I report you to the RSPCA for neglect. Dogs don't sweat in the heat like you and I. They're prone to acidosis and worse still, Azoturia."

"But—"

"Come on, let's go."

Emily pushed against the door to let Joe through ahead of her. "By the way," she said, waving one arm at him. "That goat out there is a very intelligent individual. You should—"

As the door swished shut behind them, Maggie placed five dollars on the counter to pay for her drink and pocketed the change from a nervous looking *Jean*. Then, suddenly unable to stand up any longer, she crumbled into a seat at the nearest table and laid her pounding head on the cool Formica top. Being part of a mobile vet team didn't include finding dead bodies or being stuck in a truck-stop diner miles from civilization waiting to be questioned by the police. Did it?

By the time Maggie decided that the worst scenarios a vet should encounter were to be chased by a hostile bull or maybe bitten by an angry goanna, she'd sculled her drink and dropped the empty bottle down the garbage chute. Only then did she take a deep breath and push the heaviness in her chest aside. This murder had zilch to do with them. Zilch. When the police arrived, she'd give them her statement then she and Emily could continue on their way, meet up with Craig Benham, their client, and perform their vet duties at the opening of the Kangaroo Downs race-track.

Exactly as planned.

That's when an ashen faced Joe, with a subdued Emily in tow, stumbled through the open doorway. Joe's movements appeared jerky as though a master puppeteer pulled his strings.

"Well…did you recognize the man in the restroom? Has he been here before? Is he a local?"

"He-he's dead." Like a man wandering in the desert for days, Joe stared at Maggie as though she was a mirage and he suspected she wasn't real.

Even Emily looked like she needed a drink. And something a lot stronger than Evian water. "Maggie," she said, and a worried frown creased her forehead. "Joe said the dead guy in the restroom is Craig Benham."

A gasp came from behind the counter followed by the sound of glass breaking as it hit the tiled floor. All eyes turned to Jean who immediately gave a low moan and disappeared into the back room.

"Craig Benham? Our client?" Maggie couldn't get her head around this new piece of information. Turned all her previous reasoning upside down.

Emily nodded.

"But he was supposed to meet us at the race track."

"Maybe he decided to meet us here so he could take us to the track personally."

"And then he pissed someone off real bad and his trip to the loo was interrupted by a bullet?"

Their eyes met. Maggie shivered at the unanswered questions in her friend's eyes. Was it in their best interests to forget this assignment? Forget the opening of the new track and get the hell out of Kangaroo Downs?

Get as far away as Emily's little Elf-mobile could take them?

8

Who Killed Craig Benham?

Emily dropped into the nearest chair, arms wrapped around her chest. Okay, she dealt with dead animals at the Equine clinic, but the body in the restroom was once a living breathing man. A man she'd actually exchanged pleasantries with over the telephone. A man with a name…

Craig Benham.

Her head whirled, her mouth felt dry and she could see her own confusion mirrored in Maggie's eyes. Why did she offer to go with Joe? Why did she think a second viewing of that poor man would be easier than the first? It was ten times worse.

"Does this mean we're in danger too?" Maggie's words made Emily's mind whirl faster. "After all, Craig Benham hired us to come to Kangaroo Downs. Does his death have anything to do with hiring us?"

"Don't let's jump to conclusions," Emily told Maggie more to reassure herself than anyone else. "Craig's death isn't necessarily related to the opening of the race track. Who knows, he could have borrowed a large amount of money from someone and welched on the repayments. Or, it could be a case of mistaken identity." A bubble of hysteria rose in Emily's throat. She pushed it down and forced a nervous smile to her face. "Or even a silly lover's tiff gone too far."

Maggie's eyes goggled. "Jesus, Em, what woman blows her boyfriend's brains out just because he didn't send her roses on

Valentine's Day? And then, before his brains even dry out on her kitchen tiles, drags him into her car, drives to the Truck-stop's restrooms and arranges him artfully on a toilet seat? For a start, she'd need the muscles of a brickies' laborer to—"

"Who said the lover had to be a woman?"

That stopped Maggie in mid rant. Emily could almost see the wheels slowing to a halt in her friend's head and then setting off again in the opposite direction.

"Wonder how long poor Craig's been squatting on that toilet?" Emily mused. "Or maybe it just happened before we arrived. If so, the murderer could have been hiding in the bushes or even another cubicle watching you, Mags. Did you see anyone nearby?"

Maggie brought one finger to her mouth and worried on a fingernail. "No, but I wasn't really looking, was I? More interested in getting to the nearest cubicle in a hurry." She pulled a piece of nail off with her teeth and began chewing on another. "But I think he must have been murdered earlier in the day. There were way too many blow flies buzzing around his head for it to have just happened."

"You're right." Emily scrunched her chair closer to the table and glanced surreptitiously across at the man whose hand was currently around the throat of a VB bottle, upending its contents down his throat. "What do you reckon about the owner of this place, Joe? Could he have killed Craig Benham?"

"He seems violent enough. But why leave the evidence in his restrooms? Bit of a dumb move, don't you think?"

"Maybe he didn't have time to dispose of the body so he stashed it in a cubicle and set the engaged sign in place to keep anyone from finding it. That way it would be safe until he could drive out into the bush and dump the body under the cover of darkness." Emily shrugged. "After seeing the size of the giant bull-ants around here it wouldn't take long for Craig to be unrecognizable." She drew in a deep breath, let it out slowly while processing this thought and then shook her head. "All I can say is if Joe killed Craig, he's a damn fine actor. You should have seen his face when he stood on the cistern and looked over the top of the stall. It was the color of cream cheese well past its use-by date." And when the sickening smell of a body left in 40-plus degree heat followed them from the restroom, she'd witnessed Joe bent double, losing his lunch over a scraggly bush of sun-dried geraniums.

"Yep. A *damn* fine actor." Emily repeated, absently drawing invisible circles on the green and white Formica table top with a plastic salt shaker while watching the man they were discussing flip the *Open* sign on the door to *Closed* and then stride across to join them at the table.

"Christ!" Joe groaned as he sprawled into the chair next to her. "I can't believe my best mate Craig bought it in the ladies while Jean and I were inside the diner, working." He ran a hand through his long oily hair and then pinched the top of his nose between thumb and finger.

"Tell me, Joe," Maggie said. "What was Craig Benham *really* like? All we know is that he was the Chief Steward and manager of the new race track. What was he like as a person? Was he the sort of guy who'd have enemies?"

Joe's eyes narrowed with suspicion. "What's it to you?"

"Well, people don't go around killing other people without a reason, do they? Perhaps Craig was a drug runner or involved in some illegal activity that caused whoever to bump him off."

"Hey, Craig wasn't involved in any of that drug crap. He was my best mate. I'd know if he had any enemies."

"Must have had *one*," Maggie reminded him.

Joe sniffed and wiped his nose on the back of his hand. "Yeah, suppose so. But don't know who. Hell, Craig was a great guy. Ask around town. Everyone loved Craig." Joe glanced across at the kitchen, snapped his fingers and yelled for Jean to get her ass into gear and bring them all a coffee, before adding, "Anyway, what brings you two ladies to Kangaroo Downs?"

Before Maggie could enlighten him, Emily butted in. "We came for the opening of the track, that's all." On a scale of one to ten, a husband who treated his wife like a dog-in-training rated a score of minus ten in her books and the less he knew about them the better.

"Ha!" Joe gave a snort and slumped further into his chair. "In that case you've probably travelled all this way for nothing. Oh, Jesus," he said sitting up straighter. "I don't suppose Craig's death had anything to do with the unexplained accidents."

"What unexplained accidents?

"What do you mean?"

Joe waved one arm over the table, almost knocking off a plate of congealing chips and eggs left by a fast-fleeing truck-driver. "Hell, the Kangaroo Down's track's been jinxed from the start. Workmen falling off ladders. The starting gates sabotaged and failing to open when horses were trialing. Not to mention one of the administrators getting electrocuted when he tested the two-way radio in the stewards' room."

Emily bit her bottom lip and exchanged a frown with Maggie over the table top. A pity Craig hadn't elaborated on the track's problems when he'd hired them. If he'd mentioned *electrocuted administrator* she and Maggie would be relaxing on the deck of their boat under the shade of an umbrella with a long cool drink beside them and maybe watching the antics of fit guys on jet skis racing up and down the river. Instead of battling forty-degree heat in the bush and worrying about a killer on the loose. "And did the electrocuted administrator die?"

"Nah. Jack Hewitt's tougher'n old roofing nails. Take more than an electric current to bump off old Jack. Knocked him over though and broke his leg when he slammed into a brick wall, but he was back administrating two days later, leg in a cast." Joe scratched his head and then peered at the crud under his fingernails. "And then, there's the stuff that's gone missing—like the water pipes leading to the stables and the hose-down bay. Some rabble-rouser hijacked our new pipes when the driver got out of the truck to take a piss. This meant Craig and I had to arrange for more pipes and employ a security van to bring them here." He paused while Jean slammed three mugs of coffee onto the table before hurrying back to the kitchen. Her eyes were red and puffy as though she'd been crying, but Joe didn't appear to notice—or care.

"And then some lowlife scattered broken glass over the track and the caretaker's tractor up and disappeared a week ago. We've been at our wit's end," he went on. "So…yep…I'd say most of the top brass involved in our new track are getting cold feet."

"Can't say I blame them," Maggie mumbled.

Emily agreed. Her feet weren't what you'd call warm and toasty either after hearing the unembellished story of the saboteurs.

"So what brings you all the way out here for the track opening?"

The whoosh of the front doors broke into their conversation. Two guys, one in his teens, the other late twenties, both unshaven and wearing clothes that hadn't seen the inside of a washing machine for several months, ignored the *Closed* sign on the front door and strolled up to the counter. The younger one, skinny, with a face full of metal and a buzz cut—the older guy so hairy he could have been mistaken for a cast member from the Planet of the Apes.

"Should have locked the door," growled Joe. "Hey, you two, can't you read?" he called out.

After a quick glance at the two men, Emily answered Joe's question. "We're both veterinarians. Craig booked us to give lectures at the seminar and be on hand to vet the horses on opening day."

By this time the two young men were leaning against the counter, blatantly listening to their conversation. Joe dragged his chair away from the table and stood up, muscles bulging as he straightened to his full height of six foot plus and stomped towards them. If he'd been a cockatoo his top feathers would have been standing straight. "Left your hearing-aids at home, guys? The diner's closed."

"The door wasn't locked," Buzz Cut whined.

"But the sign said we're closed." Joe scowled.

Planet of the Apes took a step closer to Joe and smiled. A smile that didn't reach his black eyes. "Just wanted to check if your good wife, Jean, needed me for deliveries today. Or needed me for… *anything*," he said, his voice suggestive.

"No, she doesn't." Joe's fists clenched and he leant into the other man's face. "And if I had my way you wouldn't be delivering for us, let alone whatever 'anything' implies. Jean might be fooled by your pathetic James Dean impersonations, but I'm not."

"Perhaps we should ask the little lady herself?"

"I don't think so." Joe's voice took on a gravelly don't-mess-with-me timbre and if he'd been a dog he'd have bared his teeth. "Now…the police are on their way, so unless you want to talk to them—we're closed."

The skinny teenager with the metal embellishments opened his mouth to speak but his hairy mate pushed past him toward the front door. "Leave it, Bazza," he growled, his body hair bursting through every hole in his sweaty navy singlet. "We've got better things to do than waste our time in this dump."

Joe's fists rose and for a moment Emily thought he was going to knock the hairy guy straight through the plate-glass door. Instead, he thrust both fists deep into his pockets and let fly with a string of obscenities that would have straightened a curling corkscrew.

Emily exchanged an eye-roll with Maggie. This guy had huge anger issues.

Maybe he *did* murder the man in the loo and was only pretending to be his best mate to provide a muddying smoke screen.

In which case, Joe was a damn fine actor after all.

Emily found herself shaking as she lifted her coffee cup to her lips. She put the cup down, reached for Maggie's hand under the table, and squeezed.

The sooner the police arrived the safer they'd feel.

9

Questions

Emily spotted a cloud of dust rising from a four-wheel drive heading up the road toward the diner. She breathed a sigh of relief and took a calming sip of coffee. At last…the cavalry had arrived. The dusty vehicle came to a stop and a rural constable climbed from the cabin. Back ramrod straight and dressed in khaki trousers, short sleeved shirt and the standard rural Akubra hat, the constable stomped into the diner and eyed the proprietor through narrowed eyes.

"Joseph Bartolli, what's this about a dead body?" He frowned at Joe. "I've already notified the department, my deputy is outside securing the crime scene, Port Augusta station is sending out two CID detectives— so I certainly hope this isn't a wind up."

"Jesus, mate, what do you take me for?" Joe growled. "I've got me best mate, Craig Benham, dead as a side of beef in one of my restrooms, no customers to serve, and me missus having one of those secret-women's-business menopausal attacks out in the back room. If that's a wind up, I'm the swagman who jumped into the bloody billabong."

The patrolman's eyes widened. "Craig Benham? Dead?"

Joe nodded.

"Sorry, mate, just had to make sure." He took a deep breath and straightened up to his full height then moved toward the front door. "I'm going to check on the victim but I don't want anyone to leave the diner. Is that understood?"

"Well, I'm not going anywhere," said Joe.

Maggie nodded.

Emily shrugged. How could they leave anyway with two rhinoceros-sized policemen guarding the entrance?

In less than five minutes the constable was back. Although his demeanor was still abrupt and officious, his eyes betrayed his emotions. No normal person could be unaffected by the sight of someone with half their face blown off. Especially if it was someone they knew.

Clearing his throat, he pulled a notebook from his pocket and eyed the two women as he fossicked blindly in another pocket and finally brought out a biro. "I'm Senior Constable Mark Kelly and I need to record the names of every person subsequently attending and departing from the scene before and after the body was discovered."

Emily's lips twitched. "Well, that could be a problem, constable," she said standing up and strolling across the room to deposit her empty coffee cup on the counter. "When I announced the news that we had a dead body on the premises, every man woman and child immediately abandoned their truck-sized meal and took off."

The patrolman's scowl deepened. "And who are you?"

"I'm Dr. Emily Harrison of *Vets2U*," she waved one hand in Maggie's direction, "and this is my partner, Dr. Margaret Post." When he didn't respond she continued. "We were employed by the deceased."

His frown deepened. "Employed?"

"Yes. Craig Benham employed us to give lectures and provide vet checks for the horses at the opening of the Kangaroo Downs race-track this coming weekend." She shrugged one shoulder. "So, if there's anything I can do to help…"

He blinked twice, his stern expression informing her exactly what he thought of the 'help' she'd already provided, then turned back to the owner of the Truck-Stop. "Joe, why didn't *you* stop your customers from leaving?"

"Stop them?" echoed Joe, incredulous, his mouth agape at the suggestion.

Determined not to be ignored Emily smiled, all sweetness and cream. "Constable, have you ever attempted to stop a tsunami?"

Constable Kelly's face reddened and Emily blinked when one hand strayed to his accoutrement belt where a gun, radio, some sort of spray, handcuffs, and a retractable baton lurked. Huh? Maybe she'd better control her remarks. Maybe constables shoot first and ask questions later out here in the Australian bush.

"It was very unwise of you to inform anyone but the police about the presence of a body, Dr. Harrison," he went on, his steely gaze boring through her until she finally lowered her eyes to his dusty black RM William's boots. "Now," he went on, swiveling his attention to Maggie and Joe. "Who found the deceased?"

Maggie lifted one hand and gave a tentative two-finger wave. "That'd be me. Unfortunately."

"Full name and address, ma'am."

While Maggie gave Constable Kelly her details and went on to explain the manner in which she discovered the body, Emily took the opportunity to check out Joe's wife who was draped against the wall in the corner behind the counter. Even from this distance Emily could see there was more to the woman's condition than the menopausal hot flush Joe had suggested. By the slump of her shoulders, the deceased meant more to Jean than the loss of a regular customer at the diner. But what was he to her? A friend? A relative? Or was he someone even closer?

Emily slipped behind the counter, approached the shaken women and laid a tentative hand on her shoulder. "Jean, I'm Emily Harrison. Are you okay? Anything I can get you?"

"I'm fine," Jean muttered. Then, through eyes that were red and puffy, she shot a nervous glance across the diner at her husband who was deep in conversation with Senior Constable Kelly. Her shoulders slumped inwards. "'Bout as fine as a chicken patty in the deep fry."

Emily, as though handling a traumatized child, took the woman by the arm and led her into the back room, away from prying eyes. "Come on, let's sit here until Constable Kelly realizes we're missing from his interrogation and yells for us," she said and waited until Jean perched on a creaky wooden chair. "Now, would you like me to make you a cup of tea?"

This small act of kindness was enough to open the floodgates. "He…he's dead." Jean's face seemed to collapse in on itself and her voice was barely a croak. "Craig's dead."

She closed her eyes and Emily had to strain to hear her next words. "How am I going to get through this?"

"Jean," Emily said as she placed a teabag in a cup, filled it with hot water and then added four heaped teaspoons of sugar. "Did your husband know about you and Craig?"

"Oh God, no! Joe would kill him if he—" Her face blanched and she clung to the base of the chair, knuckles a tight bumpy ridge. "You don't think…"

"I don't know what to think, Jean." Emily placed the cup of tea on the table by Jean's elbow. "But if you want my opinion you need to pull yourself together, run a cold flannel over your face and brush your hair. Any moment from now, Constable Kelly will be asking you some difficult questions and you need to have the right answers ready for him. Also, if Joe didn't suspect something before, he'll take one look at you now and guess immediately."

"You're right. Of course." Jean lifted the hot tea to her lips, discovered her hand shaking too much to drink without scalding herself so returned the cup to the table.

"How long have you and Craig been…together?"

Instead of answering, Jean leant forward and grabbed Emily by the arm. "Promise me you won't tell anyone," she growled her fingers so deep Emily winced and tried to pull away. "Me and Craig—us being together—it's got nothing to do with any of this."

Emily regarded the woman with a raised eyebrow. Could a woman in her late forties really be this naive?

Jean frowned and let go of Emily's arm. "Craig really loved me, you know. And Joe doesn't. All Joe cares for is his precious race horses and that stupid track."

"So why stay? Why not just kick Joe to the curb and scoot?"

"You know nothing of my life," Jean snarled then turned her back and refused to discuss the matter any further.

Emily slowly made her way back to the others. Was Jean really as naive as she sounded? Scared of her husband's anger? Or was she covering up something more sinister? And what about Joe? If he guessed his wife was having an affair with his best mate, he had motive as well as opportunity to pull the trigger.

But the big question was…did Joe care for his wife enough to risk going to jail for her?

She glanced out the diner window at Goat and his friend, the big chestnut horse. They were both munching happily on the few tufts of dry grass pushing through the mud near the water trough. Their companion, the pretty bay with the black mane and tail stood dozing under the tree, flicking his tail at the flies. Life was so much simpler for animals. No need to worry about making enough money to pay the mortgage. No need to put on a brave face to the outside world. No need to dress up to firstly attract and then hang onto your husband….

"Dr. Harrison?" Senior Constable Kelly's authoritative bark broke into her thoughts. "Would you please sit down over here? I haven't finished questioning you yet."

With one last wistful glance outside, Emily gave the policeman her best syrupy-sweet smile, strolled across the diner and arranged herself on the chair next to Maggie.

10

More Questions

Maggie shouldered her way through the front door of *Joe and Jean's Diner* and made a beeline for the Elf-mobile. What had started out as a half hour break to enjoy a truck-sized meal had metamorphosed into a truck-sized number of police uniforms, plain clothes detectives and two hours of repetitive interrogation.

"You okay to drive the rest of the way, Em?"

"Of course."

"Good. I'm so tired I'd likely run us both up the nearest tree." Maggie pressed the button on the car's unlocking device then tossed the keys to Emily. "Been thinking," she said opening the passenger side door and squeezing herself into the car. "If only I'd squatted behind a bush instead of going to the loo, none of this would have happened. Instead, we'd be settled into our B&B in Kangaroo Downs by now—maybe even having a quiet drink…or three."

"But Craig Benham would still be dead."

Maggie wrinkled her nose. Of course he would. She let out a sigh that seemed to come from right down in her toes. Their client was dead and so was the agency's first assignment. "What now?" she asked lifting one eyebrow at Emily. "Do we turn around and go home with our tails between our legs or continue on to Kangaroo Downs and find out if our services are still required?"

"It's a team decision, Mags. We're in this together. We could get the hell out of Dodge and wait for our next assignment, but if Craig's death doesn't affect the opening of the track, we're still contracted by the race-track committee."

"I guess."

"Plus, I'd like to hang around and find out what the heck is going on in this bizarre little country town. I hate quitting." Emily grinned. "Quitting gives me hives."

"We mightn't get paid for our services if the track doesn't open."

Emily shrugged. "True."

Maggie frowned. Okay, quitting might give Emily hives, but to Maggie, continuing with their present assignment was also about restoring her own confidence. Emily had given her this chance to prove her worth and she didn't want to let her friend down. "Oh, hell, why not?" she said glancing down to do up her seatbelt. "At least it will keep Constable Kelly happy as he *did* order us to stick around. Why, I don't know. I've already answered a trillion questions." Maggie reached down onto the floor for her water bottle and undid the lid. "After his interrogation I now know what it feels like to be pulled through a car-wash backwards."

Emily laughed. "The guy certainly is a control freak."

"Guess he's just doing his job."

As Emily turned the key in the ignition, two more official looking cars swung into the diner's car park. "Blimey! Who's this then?" she said. "They'll have enough cops here soon to hold a Policeman's Ball."

"That's the CSI and the PES." When Emily looked blank, Maggie explained. "Crime Scene Investigation and Physical Evidence Section. They're here to collect evidence and take photos and video footage of the crime scene."

"I keep forgetting your Greg used to be one of them. Okay, in that case, let's get going before someone else decides they want another happy snap of you with the deceased." Emily jammed her foot on the accelerator and gunned the car out of the car park and onto the main road leading to Kangaroo Downs.

"Hey, Mags," Emily said once the diner was out of sight. "Do you want to hear an interesting piece of the puzzle connected to Craig Benham's murder?"

"Yeah, shoot." Ugh! Bad choice of words. Immediately a picture of the hole in Craig Benham's face flitted through her mind. She closed her eyes and leant her head back against the headrest.

"The deceased and Jean from the diner were having an affair."

Maggie's eyes shot open. "You're having me on."

"Nope. Didn't you notice how cut up Jean was when she brought us our coffee?"

"I assumed it was because Joe spoke to her like she was his personal slave. You know…Me Tarzan, you Jane, and if you don't get your ass into gear pronto, I'll dock your grocery money and chain you to the kitchen sink."

"Maybe that's the reason she turned to Craig."

"And what? You think Joe found out about the affair and plugged a hole in the boyfriend's head?"

"It's possible."

"Only one thing wrong with that theory, Em. Why would Joe leave Craig's body in his own restrooms? Wouldn't that implicate him as the killer? If Joe was jealous of Craig and shot him, wouldn't he be more likely to stash the body as far from the diner as possible? Maybe even in the next State?"

"Or he could have left the body there to throw suspicion *away* from himself. You know, like the police might think the same as you did."

Maggie wiped a hand across her forehead. The air-conditioning in the car hadn't kicked in properly yet which made it far too hot to ponder the mangled reasoning of a killer.

"And there's one other thing I can't work out–"

"Only one?" broke in Maggie, still massaging her temples. "Lucky you…"

"How did the murderer lock the stall from the inside and then get out again without opening the door?"

"Hmm…sounds like one of those 'locked room mysteries'." Maggie shrugged. "I don't know. Perhaps he or she climbed over the top."

"But to do that, he or she would need to stand on the toilet seat and lever themselves over the top of the stall. Yet Craig was sitting on the seat."

Emily had a valid point. "Hmm…" she mused and leant back, more relaxed. At last the air-conditioning was doing its job, cooling the car. She closed her eyes and listened to the tires hissing on the hot bitumen road. "And I guess someone skinny enough to lie on the floor and wriggle under the door wouldn't be strong enough to drag Craig into the stall in the first place."

"Unless she lured him into the cubicle by calling out and saying she was hurt and then shot him when he came in."

"She? I thought you favored Joe as the killer."

"Changed my mind. I think Joe is too wrapped up in his own world to notice his wife shampooing her hair or applying extra make-up for the 'other' man in her life."

"The killer couldn't have been a woman."

"Why not? If it was a male, wouldn't he drag the body into the *men's* restroom?"

"Not necessarily. He could have used the female restroom so the police would *suspect* a woman."

"Huh. Sounds like a typical man." Emily's fingers tightened on the steering wheel and she scowled at the grey ribbon of bitumen stretching into the horizon. "Men never take responsibility for their actions. Never accept that they're in the wrong. It's so much easier just to blame the little woman."

Suspecting Emily was stoking the fire ready to chuck her husband, Peter, on the barby again, where she could prod him with sharp instruments while waiting for him to sizzle and burn, Maggie quickly changed the subject. "Did I tell you Judy rang while you were in talking to Jean? She's representing Trinity College in an Interschool showjumping competition next month. Said her horse, Alex, performed like a champ in the try-outs."

"Why wouldn't Judy represent her school?" Emily shrugged dismissively. "We all know my talented niece will ride for her country at the Olympics one day. Trinity's lucky to have her. But did I tell you what Peter's lawyer said when I—"

"Hey, Em, stop the car!" Maggie braced her hands on the car's console and squinted through the windscreen. "There's something or someone lying in the middle of the road."

"Holy Toledo!" Emily slammed her foot on the brake, swerved wildly and came to a skidding halt in the dirt. "Not another body!" she gasped. "What the hell's wrong with this town? Is the heat driving everyone insane?"

11

Jackson the Joey

Wedged in the car like cheese on a toothpick, Maggie pushed and wriggled, until, although almost falling on her knees, her feet hit the ground running. Her headache had returned. It banged away inside her skull and she had to keep telling herself that at least this body wasn't human. "It's a red kangaroo," she told Emily. "Macropus Rufus." She sighed when she drew closer to the bleeding mess and realized the poor creature was beyond their help. Looked like its neck had been broken and blood covered the open gash across its back.

Emily stared down at the animal, her mouth set in a grim line. "Whoever did this couldn't even stop to drag her off the road?"

Maggie agreed but also realized it might have been a little old lady who had neither the strength nor the nerve to get out of her car and dispose of the body. Also the car would have a huge dent in the front and would probably be leaking water all the way to the town's closest mechanic. "Okay, you grab one leg while I take the other and see if we can drag the poor creature onto the side of the road and up into the bushes," she said. "Can't leave her here or there could be a bad accident."

"Remind me never to wear high-heels in the country again," said Emily as she crab-walked across the road. "Can't even take these boots off and go barefoot 'cos the bull-ants around here are the size of small dogs."

The kangaroo was a large adult female and in its lifeless state, weighed a ton. By the time they'd dragged her off the road and under the shade of a large peppercorn tree, they were both gasping for breath.

"Well, that's another good deed for the day." Emily squatted on a stone the size of a dinosaur's head and fanned her face with one hand. "If we were part of a Girl Scout troop we'd be top of the class."

Maggie watched the ever-moving giant bull ants already at work on the dead kangaroo. It broke her heart to see the ants feasting but they had no shovel and even if they did it would be impossible to dig a hole large enough to bury an animal of that size. Under the top layer of fine dust, the ground was like cement. "Bloody ants," she snarled.

Emily shrugged. "Hey, they gotta eat too."

"Scoot over." Resigned to the forces of nature—as unpleasant as they were—Maggie plonked her large rear-end on the boulder beside Emily. The business of finding a dead man, combined with dragging a dead 'roo across the road, had taken its toll. Her back ached, her head throbbed, and she could feel her heart playing bongo drums in her chest. Maybe…just maybe…it would take more than replacing ice cream and chocolates with salads and fruit to get her body back to full fitness.

Emily nudged her with a sharp elbow, jolting her from her thoughts. "Behold!" she declared in a mock-pompous voice and indicated with her head. "I think we've finally reached the end of the yellow-brick road."

In front of them, a little below where they were sitting, was a large wooden sign. Maggie tilted her head to read the words, 'Kangaroo Downs Race-Track' painted in a bilious shade of yellow against the raw untreated wood. The sign was lopsided, as though a dwarf and a giant had stood one on each side of the sign and hammered it into the ground to their own specifications.

"Typical bush track," said Emily.

Maggie studied the race-track behind the sign and nodded her agreement. The course, cut from virgin bush, stretched out over at least twenty acres. With a racing surface comprised of packed-down dirt, Maggie guessed the horses must become almost invisible on windy days due to the dust. Overlooking the track, a grandstand fashioned out of heavy local timber and cement blocks had been painted the same bilious shade of yellow as the sign, the trimmings a deep shade of Heritage green. And the only other buildings appeared to be a large sprawling bar, a tote for the punters and four basic rows of open-air stalls for the horses.

Near the winning post and just off the track itself stood a judge's stand and what looked like a spindly ladder leading up to the broadcast box on top, so high the broadcaster would need strong legs and a nose that didn't bleed in the rarified air to reach his aerie-in-the-sky. Maggie reckoned the broadcaster would need to take his lunch, dinner and thermos with him on his one and only trip to the top on race-day. And as for getting down again on that skinny ladder—the thought made her stomach do a flip-flop and run and hide in her rib cage.

"Not what you'd call another Flemington or Rose Hill."

Emily let out a loud laugh and her eyes twinkled. "No…but like most outback tracks, the boozer appears to be the most prominent building. It's where all the happy owners, trainers and punters congregate before, during, and after each race." She stood up and tugged her chemise away from her body. "Tell you what—I wouldn't mind a cold beer myself right now. Come on, Mags. Let's go find our B&B and knock over the mini-bar. See how many cold VB's are stashed in their fridge. And if it's a teetotal mini-bar, we'll go walkabout and find the local watering hole."

"I'll be in that." Maggie licked her dry lips then cast a last glance at the race-track and frowned. Was that someone in scruffy jeans and a tank top hiding behind a bush a few meters from where two deliverymen were unloading barrels and crates of beer from a truck and trundling them into the bar ready for opening day? Eyes half-closed against the glare, she shaded her eyes with her hand to get a better view. The person behind the bush was definitely male and when one of the deliverymen glanced in his direction he threw himself flat onto his stomach and lay still. What was he up to? Why was he hiding? "Hey, Em, isn't that the skinny kid from the diner?" she said, recognizing the whiney teenager with the face full of metal and a buzz cut.

"Yes, it is. And he's acting like he's up to something." Emily took a step forward. "Hey, you!" she yelled.

Maggie grabbed her by the arm and pulled her back. "Hang on a minute, Em. Let's just wait and see what he does."

"Okay, but where's the other bloke? You know, the goon who was with this one at the diner?" Emily stole a quick look up and over her shoulder, as if expecting the big hairy guy to drop down on them from the branches of the peppercorn tree.

Emily had a point. Where *was* the other guy? Thinking of him, Maggie remembered how he radiated menace with every word he spoke, every nuance of his body language. Definitely not the sort you'd want to run into at night in a dark alley. Or, for that matter, during the day on the side of a deserted bush road.

Immediately Maggie became conscious of every sound around her. The sharp intake of her breath, the whine of the hot wind blowing in her face, a flock of white cockatoos screaming as they passed overhead…

…something skittering beside her foot.

Frozen, heart thudding against the wall of her chest like she'd just completed a hundred-meter sprint, Maggie goggled at the ground, where a lizard, neck frilled, eyes on fire, paused momentarily to hiss its extreme displeasure at her, before continuing on its way.

Her breath whooshed out in a sigh of relief and, shaking her head at her jumpiness, she squinted across at the young man ensconced behind the bushes. Maybe she and Emily were creating something out of nothing. Maybe the kid was just lying there under the shade of the bushes watching the activity at the track.

"So, if we're not going to flush him out," Emily growled. "What do we do? Wait until he's made his move and then grab him, or ring the police now?"

"Oh God, no! Not the police! Not *more* questions." Maggie groaned at the thought. "I say we leave him to it and hightail it out of this sun." When Emily frowned and went to butt in, she continued. "Look, he's just a kid. What's the most he's going to do? Wait until the deliverymen drive off and then sneak in and pinch a couple of bottles of beer from the nearest crate?" Maggie dragged herself up from the rock. She was tired. Drained. And all she wanted to do was drive to their B&B and throw herself into the nearest armchair.

"Okaaay. If you're sure." Emily didn't sound so ready to give up the idea of grabbing the Buzz Cut kid by the ear and explaining to him in great detail the error of his ways. "But I still say we should ring the police."

Maggie, wilting under the hot sun, dragged herself toward the car, stopping as she passed the dead kangaroo to flick away some greedy ants making a meal out of the kangaroo's dead glazed eyes. As she bent over, a tiny head popped out of a pouch in the middle of the 'roo's stomach.

"What the –"

"Oh, my, God!" said Emily, her face alight with smiles. She shoved herself off the tree she was leaning against and rushed forward. "It's a baby joey." She brushed ants away and carefully slid the tiny baby 'roo from its dead mother's pouch. "A baby Macropus Rufus," she crooned, cuddling the four kilo kangaroo against her chest and tucking its skinny back legs and tail under one arm.

"Seems okay," said Maggie, checking the joey out with gentle fingers. "No broken limbs, no cuts and abrasions, no bleeding from the nose or mouth." She gently felt both of the joey's feet. "Feet aren't cold so his temperature is okay."

"Poor little orphan baby," crooned Emily. "How on earth did you survive the car crash in one piece?"

"And more to the point," said Maggie, shaking her head at the bundle in Emily's arms. "What the heck are we going to do with him?

We can't sneak a baby kangaroo into our B& B."

"Yes, we can. This is a country town, Mags. It's not like we have rooms at the Savoy." She kissed the top of the baby roo's head. "Don't worry, Jackson. We'll take good care of you."

The joey's huge black eyes, wide and frightened, gazed up at her as though he understood every word she'd said.

"Oh God, she's given the joey a name." Maggie gave a mock moan. "That means we're doomed, hooked, committed to five hourly feeds plus burping." She ran one finger gently down the joey's tiny face and smiled. "As long as you understand, right now, Junior, I'm not putting my hand up for any late-night feeds."

12

Lola Brigetta

The fodder store on the outskirts of Kangaroo Downs appeared to be from another century. Giant round hay-bales and bags of chaff were stacked roof high, while everything from mediaeval rat and possum traps to dusty blacksmith's tools lined the shelves.

Maggie eyed the rusty galvanized iron and wooden maze surrounding them and rolled her eyes. "Unless we locate a human soon it could take a couple of days to find what we're looking for."

"Better mark our path with bread crumbs or chalk marks. We could get lost in here and never find our way out again."

At that moment, a Hugh Jackman look-alike wearing an Akubra hat, fringed leather jacket and stained moleskins with a knife strapped to the belt leapt from a stack of hay and stood, hands on hips, head thrown back as though he'd been transported from a Mills & Boon romance cover. "Afternoon, ladies. I'm Dion," he said in a voice that could have turned stones to melted honey.

Maggie stifled a giggle as Emily eyed Dion in bemused awe. Although a little embarrassed to be ogling the guy, Maggie agreed with Emily's assessment. After all, not every day your eyeballs were given the chance to survey such a hot specimen of manhood.

"Um…hi Dion," said Emily,

"Bonza day to be out and about." As Dion bent to lift a bale of hay from the ground as though it were a packet of marshmallows, Emily's eyes widened appreciatively. He threw the hay on top of the stack, wiped his hands on his moleskins and upped the wattage of his grin. "Now, can I be of any service to you two beautiful ladies or would you rather browse the merchandise."

Maggie could see that Emily, glassy eyed and weak-kneed, would definitely prefer to 'browse the merchandise', so she stepped forward and smiled up into two twinkling blue eyes. "Afternoon, Dion," she said. "Don't suppose you have Vytrate, Biolac and a 100ml baby bottle? Oh yeah, and a couple of suitable teats for a baby kangaroo to suck from?"

"Ah, you've rescued a joey," he drawled. "We get quite a few locals in here with orphaned joeys. Speeding cars and wild animals don't mix and kangaroos seem to be the main casualty." He moved into the next aisle and reached up to the top shelf to bring down two containers. As he stretched, his fringed jacket rode up, displaying lots of tan skin and a beautifully sculpted six-pack. Emily's breath caught in her throat. "We have Vytrate but don't stock Biolac," Dion said and handed two containers to Maggie. "But Wombaroo is a similar milk replacement for wild animals."

And then he bent down to the bottom shelf, stretching the seat of his moleskins firmly across his peach shaped butt causing Emily to sit down on a nearby hay bale. "And here's a container of Vytrate, a 30ml bottle and a packet of teats. We also have a selection of cotton pouches if you're in the market for one."

Rolling her eyes at Emily who was busy fanning herself, Maggie nodded at Dion. "Hey, I'm impressed by your knowledge of orphaned Macropods."

"All in a day's work," he said and his smile could have marketed any brand of toothpaste in the land.

At the cash register, Dion scooped their purchases into a large brown paper bag and along with the parcel, slid a brightly colored card across the counter. "Seems like you two lovely ladies know what you're doing but unless you want to be stuck feeding the little blighter every four or five hours, give Jimmy Black from Wild Life Rescue a ring. They're only forty miles outta town and ol' Jimmy'll be happy to drop by and take the joey off your hands."

"Forty miles? Hmm…bit far."

"Nah." He tossed his head, drew his knife from his belt and after cleaning it with a rag, thrust the knife back into its sheath. "Just a stone's throw up the track."

"Oh, right." Maggie glanced at Emily who was eyeing the muscles in Dion's arms like she wanted to lick them. A lot of help she'd been. "Well…thanks for everything. We really appreciate your help." She picked up the parcel and pocketed the card. When Emily didn't move she grabbed her by the arm and dragged her toward the open door. "But we must be going now. Things to do. Places to see…"

"Wow!" said Emily as Maggie bundled her toward the car. "That guy should be in the movies. Did you see the shape of his backside under those moleskins when he bent over?"

"Couldn't help but see. He stuck his caboose right under my nose."

"Yeah, and what about the size of his knife?" She let out a deep breath of appreciation. "Dion Whatever-His-Name-Is can protect me from the bad guys any day of the week."

"I thought you were off men."

"Oh, I am. I am. Completely." Emily appeared to shake herself and then grinned. "But *that* wasn't a man—*that* was a mirage."

They both laughed and while Maggie squeezed herself in behind the wheel of the Echo, Emily checked on Jackson who was happily ensconced inside one of her jumpers. The jumper had been turned into a pouch by tying the arms and neck into a knot and hanging it up on the car door. "You okay in there, Jackson?" she said.

When the baby roo's head popped out from the temporary pouch, Emily smiled. "You're lucky, little fellow. Everything we needed for you was sitting on the shelves of the fodder store."

"Reckon we'd find Methuselah's first baby tooth on one of those shelves if we looked hard enough," said Maggie as she drove the car out onto the main road leading into town. "Now, where's this B&B? I'm ready to collapse."

"Not before we rustle up something tall cold and alcoholic," said Emily, leaning into the car's air-con.

"Ooh yeah. *And* give Wild Life Rescue a ring. They can care for a baby kangaroo much better than we can."

"But—"

"Emily, we can't take Jackson around in the car with us—it's too hot. And we can't come back to the B&B every four hours to feed him. And what about the long trip home?"

"You're right." Emily gave an embarrassed laugh. "Guess I've grown attached to the little tyke."

"He is cute," Maggie agreed and then grinned. "But aren't you forgetting something?"

"What?"

"Can you imagine a kangaroo living on a boat?"

"Good point."

Kangaroo Downs was like many other Australian country towns with buildings, mostly built last century, sprawled on both sides of the one main street. Little specialty shops, a nineteenth century Emporium, a few houses, the Kangaroo Downs' pub and a garage straight from the sixties which advertised both petrol and chicken feed.

Slowing down to study the numbers on the buildings as they passed, Emily frowned. "Hey, did you see a face peering through the window of that house? And look at those three women gathered on the street corner. They're pointing at our car and talking. And the guy in shorts and a big straw hat filling his car at the garage…he's staring at us. What's going on?"

"It's a small country town, Em, and we're outsiders. I guess nothing much of interest happens around here and when strangers invade their town it gives the townsfolk something to talk about. Wouldn't get my knickers in a knot if I was you—we're only here for three days."

Three quarters of the way down Main Street, Maggie pulled up and parked the car in front of Number 96. "*This* is it?" she said switching off the engine and peering through the window at their lodgings for the next three days. "You've gotta be joking."

"Hey, don't shoot the messenger. I booked us into the only B&B in town. *Emu Bottom Bed and Breakfast.*"

Maggie took in the ancient stone building with moss growing over the exterior and a large shiny bronze plaque fixed to the wall beside the front door. The plaque informed anyone foolish enough to knock, that The Rev. Archbishop Percival Brown unveiled the Kangaroo Downs Catholic Church on 5th November 1890. "But it's a church!" she yelped. "How come you booked us into a church?"

"It's not a church now, Mags. It's a Bed and Breakfast."

"Okay, but if we're greeted by a nun in a long black habit, white winkle and the face of an angel, I will not be happy. I'm too tired and grumpy to cope with serenity and goodness. What I want is a very large whisky—not muted church music and a cup of herbal tea." She opened the car door and wriggled until her feet hit the ground. "You should have booked us into the local pub."

"I thought this would be quieter."

"What, with the residents of the little church cemetery over there partying all night long?"

"Mags, behave yourself," said Emily with a mock frown as she unhooked the jumper holding Jackson from the car door. "The church was converted into a B&B five years ago and you won't find a nun or a priest in *cooee* of the place. Now, I'll drape this jumper over my arm and the proprietor will never know there's a baby kangaroo inside."

"Oh yeah? And I've also heard there are fairies at the bottom of the garden."

After a tentative knock Maggie stood back and held her breath. She couldn't get the image of a black robed nun out of her head. However, when the door swung open with a whoosh, she almost bit her tongue. Emily was spot on. Not only was the inside of the building unlike a church—with its ostentatious hippie colors and walls decorated with flowing material and weird creations made of leather, cane, and bits of wire—but the large imposing woman in her early sixties leaning against the door jamb was as far removed from a nun as a gaudy red light district madam. Long flamboyant multi-colored dress, unlit cigarette protruding from the side of her mouth, deep lines in a face plastered with thick makeup and hair dyed the color of brass.

"G'day, ladies," the woman said in the deep gravelly voice of a six-pack-a-day smoker.

"Hi, I'm Emily Harrison and this is my colleague, Maggie Post. We booked a room for three days." Emily held out her small hand which was immediately swallowed and shaken by the other woman's pudgy, black-taloned paw.

"Darlings, I know who you are. You're the lucky ladies who found Craig Benham at the diner." The woman smiled a lazy smile, the cigarette still clamped tightly between her teeth. "Having his last crap, so I heard."

Maggie opened her mouth—couldn't think of one sane thing to say in reply to that last remark—so closed it again.

"Sorry about that," went on the woman with a cheerful wink. "We don't get a lot happening in Kangaroo Downs, so gossip's our staple diet."

"Um…" said Emily surreptitiously pushing one small furry head back into the jumper.

"You know," went on the woman, sucking away on her cigarette like it was a boiled sweet. "I came here five years ago looking for peace and quiet, but sometimes peace and quiet can come back to bite ya on the bum." Her smile quirked the corners of her mouth. "However, since you two lovely ladies arrived, gossip's rife and the phones haven't stopped buzzing. The town's alive again." She bit deeper into her unlit cigarette. "Tryin' to give up," she explained, removing the mangled cigarette from her mouth and dropping it into her pocket with a sigh. "This givin' up smoking after twenty years is a bitch. But these days people treat you like a serial-killer if you're a smoker. Plus, the doc is always on my back…so…this is my eighth attempt to beat the monster. Best so far. Been clean for three days." Her smile widened and she stepped aside to let them pass. "Anyway, enough of my yackety-yak. Come on in, ladies. I'm Lola Brigetta, the proprietor of this cavernous abode, where the cold wind sweeps under the doors in winter and freezes anything not covered with thermal underwear. Heavenly in summer though, as you've probably noticed. About 40 degrees out on the streets and barely 30 inside. No need for air-conditioning."

"Lovely place you have here," said Emily, jumping in the moment the woman paused for breath.

"Thank you, darling." Lola's eyes sparkled with pride. "The B&B is an ongoing creation of mine. Taken me five years to convert and it's a continual drain on my money and time—but I love the place. Even boasts its own ghosts."

Maggie's neck prickled and she glanced over her shoulder. She *so* was not a fan of anything in white sheets. "Ghosts?"

"Don't tell me you're afraid of things that go bump in the night?" Lola shook her head, beads clanging like a wind storm as they leaped up and down, along with her three extra chins.

"How can I be afraid of something I don't believe in?"

"Aaha." Lola's eyes twinkled and she smiled at Maggie. "You might just change your mind before your three days are up. Especially if the crabby old nun who hates every change I make to the place shows up and starts throwing things round. The room I've put you in is where she died. Found with a sharp crucifix embedded in her throat. Never did find the murderer. Which is why she won't go dancing off to her Heavenly abode until justice is finally done."

Maggie exchanged an eye-roll with Emily. Was there still time to high-tail it out of here and book a room in the local pub? After all, stale beer smells and drunken singing had to be better than a grumpy ghost, clanking chains, and a mad landlady.

Lola started for the stairs. "Now, ladies, follow me," she said before Maggie could think up an excuse to leave. "Your room's all ready. Only gotta shoo Mephistopheles out and it's all yours."

Maggie's heart kicked up another beat. Who was Mephistopheles? Another ghost? She frowned at the owner of the B&B. Surely ghosts couldn't be removed bodily from a room—like solid living people. And if so, she really didn't want to witness the weird stuff that would accompany any forced ghost removal. Clutching her suitcase like a weapon, she cleared her throat. "Er…Mephistopheles?"

"Rescue cat," Lola explained. "Big as a microwave. Wandered in here a few months ago and decided to stick around. Now the creature has taken over and thinks he owns the joint."

Not a ghost but a cat. Now *that* she could handle—even if said cat was as big as a microwave and shared a name with the devil.

"And don't worry about the baby 'roo you have tucked inside your jumper," said Lola relieving them of their suitcases. "I'll make sure Mephistopheles stays out of your room. If you keep the door closed at all times he'll soon get the message."

"How did you know?" bleated Emily.

"Hmm…how about—it's so hot outside you could fry bacon on the bitumen yet you have a woolen jumper that wriggles draped over your arm."

"Oh." Emily sounded like a little kid caught with her hand in the cookie jar.

"Plus Dion rang to let me know my two lady vets had arrived with a rescued joey in tow."

"Dion rang?" She and Emily had only left the fodder store less than five minutes ago. They hadn't mentioned where they were staying. Or that they were vets.

What sort of town was this?

"By the way," said Lola hefting their luggage, one under each arm, and leading them up the stairs. "Do the police have any idea who killed Craig?"

"Er…not yet," said Maggie blinking at the sudden change of subject. And then she decided to dig a little further. Okay, they'd decided to officially leave the crime solving to the police, but it never hurt to keep your finger on the pulse. Especially in an alien town like this. "Lola, you knew Craig Benham. Did the man have any enemies?"

Lola's laugh was grim as she stumped up the stairs ahead of them. "You could say that."

"Anyone who'd want him dead?"

"Good gravy, do you have an hour to spare while I write out a list?" She laughed and then shook her head. "Sorry, I shouldn't speak ill of the dead, but that guy spent a lifetime pissing people off. He'd con his own granny if she wasn't tarred with the same brush."

Maggie, already out of breath, gripped the bannister as she trudged up another three steps. "But Joe from the diner thought the sun shone through every one of Craig's orifices."

"Joe Bartolli is so obsessed with his mate Craig and the new race track he's blind to everything else going on around him—including what his wife gets up to."

"Aaah," put in Emily who, unlike Maggie, was tackling the stairs like a mountain goat. "So…you know about Jean's affair?"

"Darling, everyone in town except Joe knows about Jean's affair."

"Are you sure Joe doesn't know?" Emily frowned. "When we told Jean that Craig was dead, she fell to pieces like a stale biscuit. Even Blind Freddy could see how badly the news hit her."

"Darling, Blind Freddy can see more than Joe when it comes to his mate, Craig Benham. And you know what I think, even if he did know, he'd blame his cuckolded wife. Craig could do no wrong in Joe's eyes."

At the top of the stairs, Lola, her large bosom barely moving, came to a stop. God, the woman had to be more than twenty years older than her, yet she'd lugged both bags up the narrow twisting stair case and still looked ready to go out and lead the Bay to City Marathon. Maggie, puffing like a distressed walrus, shook her head in amazement. She blamed the three months spent grieving for her husband for her present condition. When you sprawl on the lounge every day for three months eating chocolates and devouring tubs of exotic ice-cream while watching *I Love Lucy* and *Midsomer Murders* reruns, plus every episode of day-time soap on the box, naturally your body suffers. Emily was right. Maggie needed to take charge of her life again. And if she didn't start dieting and jogging and concentrating on getting fit right now, she'd be no use to Emily, the agency, or herself.

At the moment though—all she was ready for was a sit down and a drink of something stronger than coffee.

"Right, ladies," Lola said, nudging a bag a little higher under her right arm. "If you like to wait on the landing for a moment I'll drop your luggage in your room and collect the big bad furball."

After Lola disappeared, then reappeared, cuddling what looked like a small shaggy lion to her bosom, Maggie tottered into their loft room and dropped like a sack of spuds onto the thick flowered quilt that covered one bed. "This has been one hell of a day and I'm beat."

"You're soft, that's why. Serves you right for hiding from everyone in that cottage in the middle of nowhere. You should have contacted me. I'd have come up and rescued you from yourself."

"Em, I told you, I needed to grieve. Alone." Maggie could see the hurt in her friend's eyes and hastened to add. "But I'm fine now. And that's all down to you, my best friend since kindergarten. The friend who gave me the chance to prove to myself that I am ready to move on." She put both arms around Emily and gave her a hug. "Thank you."

"Okay, okay. No mushy stuff," said Emily moving out of Maggie's embrace, but there was a huge smile on her face. "Now, while I mix up a feed of Wombaroo for Jackson, you can raid the mini-bar."

13

Cancelled

Two hours later, Emily, sustained by two small vodkas lifted from the mini bar at the B&B and one large bag of peanuts, stood in the middle of the Kangaroo Downs United Church hall. She studied her surroundings with a frown. Admittedly, the hall might be suitable for Nativity plays, choir practice and church meetings but as for a suitable location to give a professional lecture—she'd be struggling to give it a C minus.

According to their landlady, the church hall had been added in the late fifties and Emily could quite believe that. In fact, it looked like nothing had been touched since the last volunteer hammered the last nail in the roof sixty years ago.

She took a deep breath. Okay, she could do this. Maybe if she closed her eyes and drew in her most positive vibes a more suitable venue might materialize at a second inspection. "Ooooooommmmmm…." She opened her eyes. Let out a sigh. Nope. No magical transformation. The brightest feature in the room was still the vase of faded artificial roses that sat like royalty on top of a tradesman-like piano in front of the small stage.

"Not the Ritz, is it?" Beside her, Maggie, visibly wilting, hunched in front of a small pedestal fan that stuttered with every turn of the blades. She rolled her eyes at Emily then went back to opening the front of her shirt so the breeze from the fan could do its job.

"May as well give our presentation in a barren paddock." Emily wiped runnels of sweat from her eyes before placing her laptop on the table. She glanced at a number of white plastic chairs stacked against the back wall and shook her head. "Guess it's our job to set the chairs up too."

"Only if someone walks beside me carrying a fan."

At that moment, Charles Norton-Philips, the secretary of the Kangaroo Downs race-track, strutted in from the alcove in front of the hall and bestowed them with an ingratiating smile. "Everything up to scratch, ladies?"

Emily glared at him. Surely the man was joking. Surely he realized the resources at their disposal were way less than adequate?

"There's no *wi-fi*," she said struggling to keep from stamping her foot in a most unladylike manner. "How are we expected to present a PowerPoint presentation on 'Treating common tendon and ligament injuries in race horses', without the internet?" She threw up her hands in frustration and started pacing. "Does your club at least own a projector?"

"Oh yes, yes, of course. Quite a new one too." For some insane reason (probably brought on by the oppressive heat) the secretary reminded Emily of the nursery rhyme character, Humpty Dumpty, the egg that all the king's horses and all the king's men couldn't fix after he tumbled inelegantly from the wall. "Oh dear, I do apologize for our antiquity, Dr. Harrison," he continued, his bulging stomach and several chins jerking at every step as he lapped at her heels. "We only have dial-up around here—and as for wireless—probably another twelve to eighteen months on the horizon." He straightened his bow tie and sniffed, the angle of his nose suggesting something unpleasant lurked nearby. "Didn't our esteemed manager, Craig Benham, fill you in on our internet problems when he booked you for the lectures?"

"No, he did not." Emily stopped pacing abruptly and swiveled on one foot, recoiling in revulsion as the man's large well-padded stomach bumped into hers. Ugh! She back-pedaled so quickly she tripped over

Maggie's large feet.

"Careful there, Em." Stifling a giggle, Maggie grabbed her friend's arm to stop her from falling. "Don't want Charlie here to think you've been sampling the church sherry."

Out of sorts, Emily frowned at Maggie's Cheshire cat grin and stalked toward the table where she'd set up her computer and notes. If there was anything alcoholic in this church hall it would be covered in cobwebs and have turned to vinegar years ago.

"Hey, don't worry. We'll manage," said Maggie following her. "It'll be like the old days. You know, before all this high-tech stuff changed the way we communicate. You know…hands on. Talking and demonstrating with audience participation. Let them ask us questions and we'll answer them. Might even be fun."

Maybe Maggie was right. Emily sucked in a large breath and let it out slowly. She was getting herself in a flap over issues she could do nothing to change. It was just that she was desperate to make a success of their newly formed Mobile-Vet Agency, and so far nothing was going as planned. What with the murder of their client and now no *wi-fi*— the Universe was definitely lining up against them.

Emily strode across the bare floor boards towards the back of the hall. She picked up two chairs, one in each hand and turned to Charles. Setting out chairs must not be included in his job-description because he was attempting to sneak out of the hall and leave them to it. "Hey, Charles," she called out. "Tell us about Craig Benham. I guess you knew him pretty well."

"Craig? Er…of course." He hovered by the door, first adjusting his bow tie and then swiping at an invisible hair on his silver-gray suit before continuing. "Craig is…was…a successful horse trainer in Adelaide. He bought a property and shifted here about six years ago."

"So you knew him as a good mate?"

"Well, I wouldn't call him a good mate, but yes, I had quite a bit to do with him in an official capacity. It wasn't easy for us to get approval for a track here in Kangaroo Downs and Craig knew a couple of bureaucrats in Adelaide who helped push it through."

"But what was he like as a person?" persisted Emily. She walked across and handed Charles a couple of chairs to carry and went back for two of her own. "We've heard conflicting stories about the man. Some people thought Craig was a Saint and others a rogue."

"He was a good worker."

Hmm…Emily blew out a breath. Interrogating Charles was like squeezing juice from a dried apricot. "But did you *like* him or *hate* him?" she said. "In other words, why would someone want to kill him?"

Charles set the chairs down, straightened up and his eyes frosted over. "How should I know? I neither liked nor disliked the man. He was merely a colleague."

"Merely a colleague," repeated Emily. "So you wouldn't mind telling us where you were this morning when Craig was murdered?"

Charles huffed and puffed and scowled down at her. "I most certainly *would* mind."

"But why?" put in Maggie who'd ditched the chairs and was back to standing in front of the fan, arms out wide. "If you didn't kill Craig why not answer the question?"

Emily agreed. But when she looked up at Charles she could almost see chips of ice slaking off his eyes. "Because it is none of your business," he snapped. And if he'd been a cat that's about the time he would have hissed his disapproval. "You are here in a veterinary capacity—not to ask questions about a murder."

Maggie, immune to his arctic glare, was not deterred. She shrugged one shoulder as though she thought he was over-reacting. "Charles, the police will be asking you the same question."

"Why? I'm not a suspect."

"Because Craig was a colleague and until the police find the murderer, everyone's a suspect. You should have heard the questions they asked Emily and me. Especially me…I had the unfortunate luck to find the poor guy."

Charles put his head on one side and frowned down at Maggie. "Oh, that's right, you did." As Emily watched his expression change she could almost see the wheels spinning around inside his head. The wheel must have finally stopped at *Co-operation* because he sniffed, took a breath and then let it out slowly. "*If* the police question me, and I doubt they will, I'll tell them exactly where I was all morning. I have nothing to hide."

"So, if you have nothing to hide, where were you?

Charles gave Maggie another death stare. "My position as secretary of the race-club is only an honorary position," he said in a mouth-full-of-marbles voice. "My real job is Area Manager of the Northern Real Estate agency and that's where I was from 7am this morning. Now, ladies, if you don't mind, I have several important phone calls to make before your lectures begin." And with that, he spun around and strode off toward the alcove at the front of the hall.

"Thanks Charles," Maggie called out to his retreating back. "But does that mean you didn't leave the agency *all* morning?"

Emily grinned as Charles disappeared through the door without another word. "Don't think he's interested in chatting with us, Mags."

"Very antisocial." Maggie rolled her eyes as she leaned closer to the fan and undone another button on her shirt. "Plus he's left *us* to complete the seating arrangements."

*****

Five o'clock, the time appointed for their lecture to commence, came and went.

While Maggie hogged the fan, Emily went back to pacing the floor. What was going on? Where was their audience? The room, with its fifty empty chairs set out in neat rows, echoed with her footfalls.

Maggie, her cheeks red and hair limp, stood in front of the stuttering fan, arms wide, encouraging cool air to invade her sweaty armpits. She frowned at Charles who'd finished his phone calls and returned to the hall. "Are you sure the posters said the lecture started at five?"

"Positive," said Charles with a scowl. "I personally supervised the job of attaching posters to every lamp-post in town."

"Well, any idea why no-one has shown up?"

"I can't understand it." Charles pulled out his mobile phone and clicked in a number. "At our last meeting everyone was looking forward to participating in your lectures."

Maggie turned to Emily. "What do you think, Em? Shall we pack up or give our audience another five minutes?"

"It's quarter to six, so we may as well pack up. If they're not here now—they're not coming."

At that moment, Charles, mobile plugged to his ear, yellow bow tie quivering beneath his extra chins, gave an angry snort into his phone. "On whose authority?" he yelled.

"Easy, Charlie," said Maggie, touching him on the arm. "You'll have a heart attack if you don't calm down."

"I have Joe from the Diner on the phone," he said incredulity making his voice come out as a squeak. "He says both workshops have been cancelled."

"Cancelled? Who cancelled them?" Emily's stomach churned, the two vodkas and bag of peanuts suddenly refusing to play nice inside her stomach. "It might have been an idea to let us know beforehand."

"Joe says every poster in town has the word *Cancelled* painted across it in big red letters. Who could have done that?" He shook his head. "Whoever has invaded my position as secretary of this club will feel the full wrath of my displeasure. I'm the only one who has the authority to cancel the lectures." Charles, his bow tie jerking indignantly, snapped a goodbye to Joe, pocketed his mobile, and scowled at the floor.

"You do realize this is completely unacceptable," said Emily, unable to keep the disappointment from her voice. "Maggie and I have made the long trip to your town on the understanding we would be paid for two lectures as well as acting in a veterinary capacity at the track on the day of the races. Are these lectures going ahead as planned, or not?" She closed the lid of her laptop with a snap. "Either way, Mr. Norton-Phillips, I insist you reimburse us for coming."

"Yes, yes, of course, Dr. Harrison. Don't worry, I'll get to the bottom of this and tomorrow's live clinic at the track will definitely take place." Blinking owlishly, he produced his phone and began stabbing at the numbers again. "Maybe the police cancelled due to Craig's death."

"But surely Chief Constable Kelly would have contacted us."

"I'll have his badge if he's gone over my head," muttered Charles.

Emily crossed her arms and listened to Charles demanding whoever was on the other end of the line pull Kelly out of the interview room and put him on the phone, now. Charles was so up himself. Beside her Maggie's stomach gave a sudden prolonged and thunderous growl that seemed to echo around the empty hall. Momentarily distracted from their present dilemma, Emily stifled a giggle.

"Oh, God! Sorry!" Maggie, her face the color of a matador's cape, screwed up her nose and clasped her protesting middle. "I'm hungry enough to eat a cow—udders and all. Can't remember breakfast it was so long ago and with the fiasco at Joe and Jean's diner we missed out on lunch."

Emily shook her head in disbelief. "But you completely emptied the mini-bar in our room before we came here."

"I didn't eat *everything*…"

"You left me one bag of peanuts!"

Maggie grinned. "Oh well, look on the bright side. At least now we'll have time to order a meal at the pub before dining closes for the evening." She picked up two chairs and headed for the back of the room. "Come on, slave, let's get these chairs stacked."

"Kelly said he didn't cancel the lectures," Charles told them, bringing them both back to the present. "So who did?"

Suddenly Emily remembered the teenager from the diner who'd been skulking around the race track earlier in the day. The kid with the buzz cut. It wouldn't surprise her if he'd had something to do with this latest fiasco. She grabbed the Secretary's arm. "Charles, ask Chief Constable Kelly if anything was reported missing from the race track this afternoon?"

Charles spoke into the phone again and then gave Emily an odd look before imparting the latest news. "Someone smashed twenty cartons of beer, left a mess of broken glass and spilt beer all over the floor of the bar." His odd look turned into an accusatory frown. "How did *you* know?"

"Buzz-Cut," said Maggie and Emily together.

Charles blinked. "Who?"

"Tall skinny teenager dressed in tattered jeans and enough metal to set off every airport metal detector in the nation? Hangs around with a hairy guy."

"Oh, you mean Barry Sullivan? Wouldn't put it past him. Mother took off a couple years ago. Father's in jail and Barry's headed in the same direction."

Emily looked at Maggie. "That little creep was just waiting for the delivery guys to leave before wrecking the bar."

"And we gave him the benefit of the doubt."

"We?" Emily eyeballed Maggie. "Excuse me, but who said, 'Oh no, he's only a kid. Probably just waiting to pinch a bottle of beer?'"

"Okay, okay." Maggie held up both hands, palms out. "You're right. We should have marched him to the nearest police station the moment we spotted him hiding in the bushes."

"*And* I wouldn't put it past him to sabotage our lecture," added Emily. "I can just see the little maggot running around with a pot of red paint scrawling *cancelled* across all the posters."

"But what I can't work out…" mused Maggie, "is what the kid's got against the opening of the track? Why stop a project that brings jobs and people to the area? What's in it for him?"

Emily couldn't work this out either. Why would a kid of eighteen put himself in danger of being caught and jailed just to stop a race track opening in his home town? You'd think he'd welcome the attraction. She frowned at Maggie. "Could he be anti-horse racing? Or an adrenaline junkie? Or just a little piece of shit that can't bear to see others happy?" She shook her head. No, there had to be something more to his actions than that. "I know." She snapped her fingers. "I think he's working for someone higher up the food-chain. I think someone's paying him to cause havoc at the track."

Maggie nodded slowly. "I think we need to have a long chat with our young friend, Barry Sullivan. Don't you?"

As they stacked the chairs away they listened to Charles ringing around and accusing everyone of violating his authority. He seemed more put out by the indignity of someone else cancelling the lectures than the fact they were cancelled.

"Okay?" Chair-stacking completed, Emily scooped up a box of printed material and placed it in Maggie's arms. "Here, you take this. I'll carry the rest of the gear out to the car."

She looked across at Charles who'd finished making phone calls and stood surveying the empty hall. "All finished in here?" he asked.

"Guess so." Maggie's eyes raked the man from top to toe, her expression clearly adding—*no thanks to you*!

Emily's grin widened.

"Good. I'm ready to lock up now."

"So," said Emily keeping in step with Charles as they carried their equipment through the back door into the car park. "Did you find out who cancelled tonight's lecture?"

"I have no idea who undermined my authority," he answered, tone oozing with righteous pomp. He turned at the door to insert a large key in the lock. "But when I do, you can be assured, I'll complain strongly."

As they walked into the carpark, even from a distance, Emily could tell there was something amiss with her car. The red Echo seemed smaller, closer to the ground. Her stomach dropped and her breath caught in her throat as she let out a soft curse.

Maggie came to a halt beside her. "What the—"

"I don't believe it." Charles came to a stop, eyes bugged.

While Charles and Maggie stood and gaped, Emily kept walking toward the car.

The car with no wheels.

The car with the word CANCELLED painted in big red letters across the front windscreen.

14

Trapped in Kangaroo Downs

Bewildered, Maggie stared at the crippled car. The image didn't make a whole lot of sense. Why would someone go to the trouble of removing the wheels on Emily's little red Echo? Why scrawl *cancelled* across the windscreen?

To prove a point.

But what *was* the point?

Although her flight instincts screamed at her to run from whoever was menacing this close-knit outback town, Maggie's innate curiosity and indignation won the day. This unknown *someone,* whose aim was to sabotage the track, had stepped over the line when he or she chose to threaten *Vets2U'*s reputation.

She let out a sigh and scowled at the car with no wheels. It was all so confusing. There was no rhyme or reason to this latest act of sabotage. Who could possibly feel threatened by their presence? Who wanted them to leave?

And why?

Maggie could hear Charles talking to the police on his mobile. Good, at least one of them was on the ball. She certainly wasn't. And Emily was too busy swearing. It felt like they were in the middle of some police show on television and she couldn't work out where the plot was headed.

Sweat beaded on her forehead as the unrelenting sun beat down on the top of her head. When would she learn to wear a hat? Impatiently, she wiped the moisture away and let her eyes wander over the word scrawled on the windscreen in red spray paint. *Cancelled*. God knows what Emily's Insurance Company would say. Probably up her premiums.

Jaw clamped shut and face brick red, Emily squatted down beside her car. She ran the fingers of one hand over the nearest bare axel and shook her head as though she still couldn't believe the wheel was missing. "Why?" she growled and stood up, her eyes flashing. Any minute Maggie expected steam to come blasting out of her friend's ears.

Emily fisted both hands on her hips as she turned to Maggie. "I suppose you realize that until our car is fixed we're trapped in this godforsaken town?"

Maggie nodded. Of course she did—but getting angry to the point of self-combustion wouldn't help the situation.

"Trapped with both a saboteur AND a murderer," Emily added.

Hmm…there *was* that.

"Our trip to Kangaroo Downs was supposed to be a regular assignment." Emily's voice caught in her throat. "You know, present two lectures and supervise the veterinary duties on opening day." She shook her head at the incapacitated car. "Not this!"

Maggie gripped Emily's arm and squeezed. "We'll get to the bottom of this, Em. We'll show whoever's responsible, that *Vets2U* is not to be trifled with."

Emily's eyes narrowed as she watched Charles lean forward to get a better view of the writing on the windscreen. Her voice could have cut glass when she spoke. "Do you know anything about this, Charles?"

"Me?" Charles' eyes widened and for a moment Maggie thought his bow tie would ping right off the front of his shirt. "How would I know any more that you? I was in the hall the whole time."

"Not every minute," put in Emily, her tone clipped and accusatory. "You were off making phone calls most of the time."

"In the alcove at the front of the hall. I was nowhere near the car park, plus where did I put the wheels, and do you see any grease or red paint on my clothes?”

Maggie put a calming hand on Emily’s shoulder. “Of course you didn’t do it, Charles. Emily’s upset, that’s all.” She rubbed her hand up and down her friend’s back. “When you were in the alcove out the front, Charles, did you see anyone hanging around? Anyone acting suspiciously?”

“Anyone with a can of red paint?” put in Emily.

“I only had a view of the main street from the front. Not the car park entrance. That’s around the back.”

“Did you see a truck or ute or even a van? Anything suitable for stashing four car wheels?”

Charles shook his head. “As I said before, from the front alcove of the church you can only see the main street—not the car park at the rear.”

“But the church is on a corner. Did you notice anyone turning off the main road into the side street?” said Maggie. “Think hard, Charles.”

“Sorry, I was talking on the phone and not really watching who was driving past. Not that our main street ever gets busy.” He screwed up his nose in thought. “Although, come to think of it,” he said, pulling reflectively on one of his many chins, “I did notice the van from Joe and Jean’s diner out the front of the butcher shop across the road from the church. Didn’t see where it went after that because I came back into the hall.”

“Interesting,” said Maggie.

“Not really,” put in Charles. “Someone from the diner is always either delivering or picking up goods from shops along the main street. Our motto in this town is to buy local. Keeps the town afloat.”

“Still, I think I’ll zip across the road and have a little chat with the butcher. See what I can find out,” said Maggie and handed Charles the box of pamphlets she was carrying. “Can you look after these until I get back please Charles? I won’t be long.” She turned to her friend. “You be okay, Em?”

"Yeah, go on. I'll stay here and set a rocket under the police when they arrive."

Maggie squeezed Emily's hand and then took off, running.

"But-but Constable Kelly will want to speak to you," Charles called to Maggie's departing back.

"Well, he'll have to speak to me when I get back. I need to find out who was in that van."

Cursing her high heels, worn only to appear more professional while presenting her lecture, Maggie darted out of the carpark, up the side street and across the main road to the butcher shop, almost spraining her ankle as she stumbled up the curb.

A man in gray overalls leaning against the front window of the hardware shop next to the butcher's hiked his eyebrows up around his hairline. Smoke billowed from the cigarette poking from the corner of his mouth and an unpleasant smell surrounded him. "Watch it," he said, his voice coarse as gravel.

Finding it hard to breathe after her Olympic dash, Maggie staggered across and leaned against the window beside him. She opened her mouth to speak and then closed it again. Damn. She needed more air before she could talk. All those chocolates and cartons of ice cream had turned her into the Goodyear Blimp. She must be at least ten kilos overweight. First thing she'd do when this assignment was over would be to book into a gym with a personal trainer.

A minute passed. A very long minute. While the man puffed on his cigarette, Maggie concentrated on breathing—in-out-in-out—until she had enough breath stored in her lungs to force some words out of her mouth without choking and dropping dead at the man's feet. "Hi, there," she said her voice raspy as it pushed through her tight throat. "Don't suppose you saw anyone go into the church carpark, strip one of the cars of its wheels and then use red paint to write a message on the windscreen?"

"Nah," said the man in the gray overalls giving her an eye roll that clearly said, '*and when did they let you out of the asylum?*'

"Well, did you see a van stop out the front here?"

"Nah."

Maggie held in a scream of frustration. This guy with the strange odor looked as if he'd grown out of the pavement. Surely he'd seen something. "What about a truck or ute, or even a car?" At a pinch, she guessed two wheels could be hidden in the boot while the other two could be placed on the back seat and covered with a blanket. "Seen *any* vehicle near the church?"

With great concentration, the man in the gray overalls blew out a smoke ring in the shape of a squashed donut. As it rose high in the air and disappeared under the canvas awning of the shop, his eyes followed its progress. Then, evidently satisfied with his creative endeavor he looked down at Maggie and slowly shook his head. "Nah," he said. "Just came outside for a smoke. Been working out back of the hardware store fixing their septic tank." He indicated the shop next door with a lazy flick of his head. "Old Jack Hewitt, the butcher, he might of seen somethin'. Why doncha ask him?"

"Okay, thanks." Maggie took a deep breath, realized that wasn't a good idea now she knew where that dreadful smell originated from and pushed herself off the window.

As she opened the glass door and walked into the butcher shop, Maggie wondered where she'd heard the proprietor's name, Jack Hewitt. She had a faint recollection but couldn't put her finger on where and in what association.

It was the thick white cast on the man's left leg that jogged her memory. As well as the local butcher, Jack Hewitt was the administrator who'd been electrocuted while testing a two-way radio—another victim of the track saboteur. In his mid-sixties, Jack was hard at work running a saw through a leg of lamb. God they made folk tough in this part of the world. Crutches propped up beside him, Jack stood beside the saw, busy turning the leg of lamb into at least two dozen chops.

"Good afternoon," he said, his wrinkled face breaking into a genuine smile. "And what can I get you today? Some nice lamb chops? A piece of juicy steak so fresh it was running around the paddock yesterday?"

"Your meat looks first class, Jack, but I'm not looking for dinner. I'm looking for information."

"Pity. These chops would grill up beautifully on the barbecue," he said, still smiling. "But if it's info you want…ask away."

"Well, I was just wondering if you'd seen a vehicle near the church this afternoon. My friend had all her car wheels stolen and her front windscreen ruined while her car was standing in the church car park."

"Blimey. Our little town hasn't been very welcoming to you and your friend since you arrived has it? I believe you, Maggie Post, were unlucky enough to find Craig's body?"

Maggie didn't bother showing surprise at his prior knowledge of both her name and her unlucky find—the grape vine in Kangaroo Downs was stronger than a steel cable. "Yes, that was me. But I wasn't as unlucky as poor Craig."

"True." He set the chops out on a white tray, placed them on the counter beside another tray heaped with fat sausages, and then looked Maggie in the eye. "Well…let's see. I haven't noticed a vehicle hanging around, but I've been busy making up orders and struggling to master these crutches at the same time." He wrinkled his forehead. "Of course the Truck-stop van was here. It pulled up outside my shop about half an hour ago to pick up a meat order. Joe and Jean are in charge of the catering for the track on opening day."

Maggie's ears stood up and began the proverbial flap. Joe from the Diner? Well, well, well. Maybe Joe wasn't so mad keen on the race track after all. "Did Joe drive over to the Church hall after he stopped here?"

"Jean was the driver."

"Are you sure you only saw Jean? Was Joe inside the van? Could he have slipped across to the Church hall while Jean picked up the order?"

"The only person with Jean was John Taylor, known locally as Ape. Jean often employs the guy to do any heavy work at the diner when Joe's busy at the track."

Ape? Must be the big hairy guy who came into the diner with the tall skinny buzz-cut kid. Ape was the one who fronted up to Joe.

Jack shook his head. "I know where you're going with this, Maggie, but you're barking up the wrong tree. No way would Joe jeopardize the opening of the track. The Kangaroo Downs race-track is his baby."

Maggie's radar which had been lighting up like a Christmas tree sighed and went limp.

"Look, do you mind if I sit down while we talk? Leg's being a bit tricky." Jack carefully lowered himself into a nearby chair, edging his plastered leg out in front of him. "Now," he said letting out a sigh, "tell me what happened."

"You okay? Need any help?" Old Jack was tough, but it looked like he was close to passing out. No wonder. The man had put in a full day at the shop. She shook her head at him. "I bet the doctor told you to keep off that leg for at least a fortnight."

"I'm fine. Just a bit tired." He smiled up at her. "It's the cast—weighs a ton. My daughter will be back in a minute. She's been helping in the shop all day but had to go pick up the grandkids from after-school care." He stretched his leg out until comfortable. "Now, Maggie, fill me in on what's been going on over at the church."

Maggie leant against the counter on both elbows. "In a nutshell, the saboteur cancelled our lectures and when we came out of the Church hall we discovered Emily's car was minus its wheels. Charles Norton-Phillips thought he saw the van from the diner parked over here so before Chief Constable Kelly arrived and started with his questions, I came over to get a few answers." Maggie leaned closer. "Are you sure they didn't drop Joe off at the church carpark before collecting the meat order?"

Jack shook his head. "Joe wasn't in the van, Maggie."

"But he could have been hiding—"

"Joe's in custody. Jean said he was taken to the police station for questioning over Craig's murder an hour ago and he hasn't returned. Evidently, the bullet matched a rifle found nearby and registered in Joe's name. A rifle Joe swears was stolen a week ago."

"Did he report it missing?"

"Hadn't got around to it."

Hmm…so if Joe was in custody he couldn't have stolen the wheels off Emily's car. And if Joe was the murderer, it also meant the murderer and the saboteur were two different criminals. With two separate agendas. "Right." Maggie rubbed at the frown she could feel between her eyes. "Looks like Joe found out about Jean's affair with Craig and killed him in a fit of rage."

Jack pulled at his bottom lip in denial. "Joe might have been upset about the affair, but I can't see him shooting Craig because of it. They were great mates. In fact, I think he had a better relationship with Craig than he did with his wife."

"What do you mean?"

Jack shook his head and chuckled. "No, I'm not suggesting they were anything but good mates but Joe and Jean were more working partners than loving spouses."

"From the little I saw, I'd say Joe treated his horses better than his wife."

"More reason not to care if Jean had an affair—especially not enough to shoot his best mate because of it."

Maggie pushed off the counter and straightened her blouse. The air-conditioning in the butcher shop made leaving the shop that little bit harder. "Well," she said, "as much as I've enjoyed our chat, it's time for me to brave the 40-degree heat again." She noticed Jack's wince of pain as he used a crutch to push himself out of the chair. "Will you be okay? Would you like me to stay with you until your daughter gets back?"

"Don't worry about me, dear. Stephanie will be here in a few minutes and she'll drive me home. The shop's actually closed but I wanted to finish off a couple of orders while it was quiet around here." A smile lit up his face. "The town will soon be a hive of activity. You know, last minute preparations for the opening race meeting on Saturday. We've waited a long time for this."

"Well, good luck, Jack. I'll probably see you there."

"You certainly will. The lowlife who did this would need to break more than one leg to keep me away from the track opening. By the way, if you're looking for me on the day, I'll be in the judge's tower." He let out a chuckle and banged the cast with his fist. "Although with this baby, they'll probably need to hire a crane to lift me up there."

Maggie laughed. "I'll keep an eye out for the crane then." With a stiffening of her shoulders in readiness for the scorching heat outside, she made her way to the door. "I'd better get going before your rather officious country cop sends out a search party for me—every one of them armed with a set of handcuffs."

Jack's deep throaty laugh followed her as she pushed against the glass doors and stepped outside. The hot wind blasted her, smacked her in the face with its intensity and took her breath away. Geez, if she wanted to fry a couple of eggs for dinner there'd be no need of a stove. Crack the eggs on the road, wait in the shade of the shop awnings for two minutes, and voila the eggs would be ready to serve.

15

Who is the Saboteur?

Emily was ready to crash.

In the last hour she and Maggie had answered ninety-nine-and-counting questions from both Chief Constable Kelly and his junior sidekick, PC Ryan, who looked every bit of twelve years old. She'd rung her insurance company and explained their dilemma. She'd arranged for her car to be towed to the town's garage where it would be fitted with four new wheels and a new windscreen. Plus, she'd almost come to blows with the snooty Charles Norton-Phillips who seemed a bit blasé over security issues for their lecture the following day at the race track. She was freaked out that he wasn't freaking out too.

Yep. Emily was ready to crash.

As they trudged side by side down the main street toward their B&B, Maggie blew out a breath. "You know," she mused, "if the police have Joe locked up for Craig Benham's murder, at least we don't have to worry about a murderer running lose in the town while we're here."

"Guess so," Emily glanced across at her friend who was struggling to keep up. "But we still have a saboteur on the lose."

"A saboteur with a low IQ," added Maggie. "A saboteur who wants us to get out of town, yet disables our car. Pure genius. Not."

The main street of Kangaroo Down was like a lot of small Australian country towns that grew up in the early 1900s. One long street with shops and buildings on either side of the main road. No wonder the townspeople were fit. If they wanted to buy groceries, plus post a letter, the grocery store grew out of the pavement at one end of town and the post office, which also served as the dry-cleaners and the newsagent, stood at the other end.

"Of course that's only if the police have the right guy in jail," said Emily stopping to look in the window of a large furniture store where she instantly fell in love with a beautifully crafted coffee table. "Somehow, for all his bluster, I can't see Joe killing his mate."

"Jack Hewitt from the butcher shop says the police discovered the murder weapon nearby and the rifle belongs to Joe."

"But why would Joe leave the murder weapon where it could be found so easily? Wouldn't he take the rifle out in the bush and bury it or smash it up or whatever crooks do with their murder weapon?" Emily decided she'd never fit the gorgeous coffee table in the car with all their luggage, so reluctantly moved on down the street. "What if the real murderer framed Joe by shooting Craig with Joe's rifle and then left the gun near the scene of the crime for the police to find?"

"My butcher friend said Joe swears his gun was stolen a week ago but he hadn't got around to reporting it missing."

"There you go."

Maggie shivered and looked over her shoulder. "But that would mean the murderer is still out there."

"Yeah…*and* the saboteur. Unless the saboteur and the murderer are one and the same." Suddenly Emily could relate to Maggie's apprehension. Her heart kicked up a beat. She stared hard at the other people walking along the street. Geez, it could be anyone. Two young women dressed in short shorts and miniscule tops stared at her and giggled as they strolled past and when a bearded man swinging a string bag full of fruit and vegetables bumped into her, she instantly went into attack mode. Tense and on the balls of her feet she stood ready to swing her laptop at his head. Bearded guy merely doffed his battered Akubra, apologized and after giving her a toothless smile moved on down the street.

Emily closed her eyes and let out the breath she'd been inadvertently holding.

"I've been thinking," said Maggie staggering as her left heel met a hole in the pavement, "if the saboteur and the murderer *is* the same person, wouldn't that leave Joe in the clear? At the time your car wheels were stolen, Joe was cooling his heels in a jail cell."

"Mags, I don't know what to think any more."

"Oh well, thank goodness the day's almost over," Maggie said. "Now we can relax and think of food. Can't remember the last time I actually sat down and ate a meal. Geez, even a table leg covered in creamy mustard and chives would look good at the moment."

Emily couldn't raise a smile. She had a bad feeling in the pit of her stomach and it had nothing to do with food. She let out a sigh that seemed to come all the way from the tips of her toes. "The day hasn't finished yet, Mags."

"Hey," Maggie bumped against her as they walked and grinned that special Maggie grin that usually lightened her mood. "Cheer up, Em. Just think of steak and chips and salad followed by the most calorie laden dessert on the pub's menu."

"Oh, no, we forgot about, Jackson." Suddenly remembering the baby kangaroo in their room, Emily put a hand to her forehead. "Jackson's overdue for his next feed."

"No worries. I'll take care of the baby while you hop under the shower. Freshen up."

Emily cut her eyes to Maggie and frowned. What was she on about? Why did she need a shower?

Maggie let out a loud belly laugh and bumped Emily again. "You'll agree with me when you take a look in the mirror. Somehow, you've transferred grease from the car's axles onto your hands and onto your nose and both cheeks and now there's a large blob of grease on your forehead, in the shape of a legless frog."

"Why didn't you tell me before the police arrived?" Emily groaned. "No wonder PC Ryan looked as though he was stifling a giggle every time he asked me a question."

"PC Ryan is still going through his terrible twos."

Emily didn't answer. They were now in sight of their accommodation and instead of hurrying forward in anticipation, she slowed to a crawl. Oh, No. This day was about to plummet downhill and crash into a tank full of piranhas.

"Come on, Em." Maggie pulled on her arm. "Relax. Nothing more could possibly go wrong today."

"Don't bet on it," she growled and pointed with her head to a solitary figure camped on the front steps outside Emu's Bottom Bed and Breakfast.

And it wasn't their quirky landlady, Lola Brigetta.

It was the tall skinny teenager with a face full of metal piercings. The kid who'd wrecked the bar at the race track. The kid most likely responsible for sabotaging their lectures and removing the wheels from her little red Echo.

Barry (Buzz Cut) Sullivan.

16

Buzz Cut

Emily stopped dead in her tracks. This didn't bode well. Was Barry waiting to grab their handbags? Pull a gun on them? Give them a stronger message to get out of town with the help of a sharp knife? Fear froze her in her tracks.

But not Maggie.

"What the hell is *he* doing here?" Feathers ruffled, Maggie snorted then strode to the steps and glared down at the offender. "You've got a nerve, kid. What do you want?"

When Barry merely looked up at Maggie and gave a weak grin, Emily took a step forward. No sign of a knife. No sign of his big mate, Ape. She let out a breath. Still cautious, she joined Maggie and stood on the other side of their unwanted visitor. She suddenly remembered the way the teenager's eyes had run up and down her body when he winked at her in the diner. Gauging the weight of her laptop as a weapon and wishing she'd bought the heavier model with her, she produced a steely death-glare to match Maggie's. "Are you sitting here for a specific reason, Barry?"

The gangly teenager tipped his head on the side and smirked. "First up—me mates call me Bazza."

"We are *so* not your mates," said Emily, deciding the five piercings in his right ear were way overkill. "Now, unless you want me to turn the garden hose on you, answer my question."

Like all sulky teenagers, if his lip dropped any lower it would be trailing in the dirt. He shrugged. "Came to see you two, didn't I?"

"And who said we'd want to see *you*?" Maggie hovered over him like the prophet of doom. "Give me one good reason—just one—why we shouldn't hustle your sorry ass to the nearest police station? We saw you hiding in the bushes like a snot-nosed criminal earlier today, just before the bar got smashed up at the track."

"No! No! It wasn't me!" He put his hands up in the universal peace position. "I only took two bottles of beer from one of the crates. That's all. I didn't smash the place up. Everything was fine when I left. Honest." The boy sighed so deeply it shifted his bony shoulders into a defeated slump. He shook his head, the silver studs alive with movement. "It's just…sometimes I can't help meself. Bad stuff just happens around me."

"Pathetic excuse," snapped Emily, who'd heard that 'I couldn't help myself' line one too many times from her soon-to-be-ex-husband. "What are you, seventeen? Eighteen? Old enough to take responsibility for your actions. If you know something's wrong—don't do it. Simple as tying your shoelaces." Arms folded across her chest, Emily glared down at the boy. "So…as well as stealing beer, did you have anything to do with stealing the wheels from my car while we were in the church hall?"

"Or cancel our lectures with a big spray-can of red paint?" put in Maggie.

"Not me. I didn't do any of that. I know nothing about stealing wheels from your car. What would I want car wheels for? I ride a bike."

"Where were you between four and five this afternoon?"

"Here. On the steps. Waiting for you."

"Yeah, and pull the other one," growled Maggie shaking her head in disbelief.

"He's telling the truth, you know." Emily and Maggie looked up. Their landlady, Lola Brigetta, carrying several long stemmed yellow roses and a large pair of garden secateurs, appeared around the corner of the building and nodded at them. "Good afternoon, ladies," she said and dropped the secateurs into the pocket of her gardening apron. "Other than the three times he came inside for a glass of cold water, Bazza's been sitting on my steps for the last two hours."

Maggie blinked. "Hmm…well…"

"Okay, you didn't sabotage my car. But what about cancelling our lectures?" Emily turned to Barry. She wasn't ready to let up on the little toe-rag yet. "Was that you?"

"Wrong again." Lola pushed away the sweaty tendrils of hair that hung limply across her face then took out a fresh cigarette and eased it reverently into her mouth. A look of pure bliss passed across her face. "Um…" she said and seemed to shake herself to get back into the moment. "The reason no-one came to your lectures was because our local DJ announced over the radio they'd been cancelled."

"What?" Emily screeched. "And who told him?"

"Guess you'll have to ask Drake Pearson our local DJ about that."

"You can bet your last dollar I will." Emily tamped down her anger at the town's stupid-beyond-comprehension DJ and turned her attention back to the boy-most-likely-to-end-up-in-prison-before-his-twentieth-birthday. "So why *are* you here, Barry? What are you after?"

He took a deep breath as though getting ready to go into battle. "It's me greyhound, Rocky," he said. "He's hurt his foot see, and the town vet won't look at him 'cause he reckons it was me who set fire to his rubbish bins last week." Barry shook his head. "And it wasn't me. Honest. I mighta graffitied his fence—but I don't do fires." His eyes, pleading now, settled on Emily's face. "See, when my mate Ape and I were in the diner, I heard ya telling Joe you're vets."

Maggie scowled. She took a step closer to the boy with enough facial decoration to send a metal detector screaming. "So what?"

Emily tried hard to suppress a smile. She could tell by the snarl on her friend's face that if the kid on the steps made one false move Maggie would likely tie him up with his own two arms and threaten to use him for fish bait. After all, Maggie Post knew a liar when she saw one. Hadn't she put up with her lying brother, Peter, ever since he was brought home from the hospital wrapped in a baby blanket, thirty-six years ago? Emily decided it was only natural Maggie's liar radar was well tuned in.

"Thing is," Barry gulped, and slid his eyes across to Emily. "I need to pay Mr. Chang, that's the guy who owns the caravan park where I live, a wad of back rent money. He reckons if I don't come up with the three hundred bucks, like by the end of this week, he's gonna toss me out."

"And we should care about this because—?"

"Let him finish, Mags." Emily raised one eyebrow in her friend's direction. "Let's at least give the arrogant little sod sixty seconds to convince us not to hogtie him, throw him in the boot of our car, and drop him off in a cell at the Kangaroo Downs police station."

"What car?" said Lola sucking on her cigarette and smiling as though she was enjoying the entertainment. "I hear your car has no wheels at the moment."

Emily let out a sigh. Yeah. As well as being stuck in this crazy town they were stuck without a car.

The teenager's shoulders slumped even further but he soldiered on. "Look, the hot times me dog's been clocking in his trials at Port Augusta, he's a cert to win thee on Saturday. And if he does, I can pay Mr. Chang the back rent I owe him from the prize money. But if I scratch him 'cause of injury, I'll have to sell me dog to pay the rent." He ran a hand through his spiky hair making it look like he was wearing a hedgehog on top of his head.

"Shall we get the violin out?"

He cracked his knuckles and pulled a face like he'd been sucking on a lemon. "I've had Rocky since, like, he was a pup. Runt of the litter, see. No-one else wanted him, so the breeder gave him to me for working in the kennels. Now he's me best mate and I don't want to lose him."

"Maybe you should have thought of that before you 'forgot' to pay the rent."

The teenager shifted his weight onto his hands and pushed ready to stand up, but when Maggie trod on one of his fingers he quickly changed his mind and sank back into a sitting position on the step.

Maggie returned his offended scowl with one of her own. "Just sit tight kid until we've decided what we're going to do with you. Okay?"

He nodded and then fixed pleading eyes on Emily. Evidently thought she was the weak link and easier to crack. "Please, come an' look at me dog. See if you can fix him up so he can race on Saturday arvo. I don't wanna sell him—but I don't wanna live on the streets again either."

Oh God. Now the kid had that *poor me* expression on his face. With a sigh, Emily felt her resolve softening, tried to straighten her spine and think nasty thoughts, but glancing across at Maggie could see her friend, for all her intimidating stance, had been suckered in too. What a couple of marshmallow pushovers they were when it came to sob stories —especially when it involved sick or injured animals and kids whose parents had left them to fend for themselves. She let out another sigh. Wasn't that the reason she'd worked two jobs to pay her way through vet school so she could help injured animals?

Emily looked down at Barry whose body looked a lot fitter and younger than hers. Could she trust him? Doubtful. And it wasn't just because he was born with that extra chromosome that made him male. It was because she'd met his type before. He was a taker—rarely a giver. And he'd graduated with flying colors from street-smart, storytelling parents who didn't give a damn. Didn't know the meaning of responsibility. And whose main aim in life was to forget they'd ever given birth to a son.

Emily glanced across at Maggie and winked. "What do you say, Mags? Should we risk fraternizing with the town's number one villain, or should we stake him out on a bull ants' nest?"

"Hmm," Maggie hedged. "If it was up to me, I'd opt for the second alternative. Probably whistle up a couple of hungry dingoes to help the bull ants finish him off. But as I can see you're hooked on treating his damn dog, I guess we're stuck with the first."

"Okay." Emily straightened her shoulders, all business now. "Where do we find this dog of yours?"

"At the caravan park." The boy glanced nervously from one stern face to the other and squirmed. "Uh. Can I get up now?"

Emily nodded, but before the boy could move, Maggie let out a growl. "But you'd better take it real slow and easy, kid. And if this is a wind up to steal our money, I warn you, I'm no pushover. Being married to a policeman for umpteen years, I know more moves than you've had roast dinners."

Emily covered her mouth with her hand to stop from laughing. Maggie was so unfit she'd more likely end up on the ground herself if she tried one of her 'moves'. And Barry could probably count the number of 'roast dinners' he'd eaten on one hand—with the thumb bent down.

Eyes glued to Maggie, the boy slowly pushed himself to his feet and pointed up the road. "Um…the caravan park's that way. On the edge of town."

"Take my car," said Lola pointing to a silver Subaru parked on the road behind them. "Keys are under the front seat."

"We *should* feed Jackson first," said Emily.

Lola waved them on. "All done. Hope you don't mind, but I could see you were running late so I made up a bottle from the can of Wombaroo you left on the bed and fed him about half an hour ago. Cute little guy."

"Thanks, Lola. Appreciate that," said Emily. "I'll ring Jimmy Black from Wild Life Rescue as soon as we get back. Dion said Jimmy would pick Jackson up."

"Don't worry, I'll give Jimmy a ring while you're away."

Emily strode to the Subaru, threw open the passenger side door and looked back at the ungainly teenager. "Okay, Barry, get in the car. I'll drive. Maggie can sit in the back seat and you can travel in the passenger side next to me. I still don't trust you, so that way we can both keep an eye on you."

Maggie gave a mock growl. "Can't see why he shouldn't travel in the boot of the car."

"I swear I won't try anything." The boy quickly slid into the passenger seat before Maggie could carry out her threat. "I promise."

"Barry," Emily said sending him one of her most disdainful looks—the one she usually reserved for sleazy salesmen, "just fasten your seat belt and zip your lips. I'll drive you to the caravan park and take a look at your dog, but your assurances mean nothing to me. In fact, I wouldn't trust one of your *promises* if it came in a box of Haigh's chocolates and was tied with a red ribbon."

17

Red Paint

The caravan park, set on a flat scrubby piece of land on the outskirts of Kangaroo Downs, was a mixture of old and new vans with half a dozen permanent cabins, a shower block and an adventure playground for the kids.

Bazza's van, resting on a pile of crumbling cement bricks, looked at least sixty years old. Sixty years of sun, rain, and neglect which had weathered the exterior to a depressing all over gray color. In contrast, the mass of bright red geraniums jostling for sunlight in a long wooden box along the front of the van appeared welcoming.

"Are you the one with the green fingers?" Emily asked as they climbed from the Subaru and approached the caravan door. "Or do you live here with a garden enthusiast?"

"Nah. Just me and Rocky." Evidently embarrassed by the compliment, he shrugged. "Geraniums are easy to grow."

A white and black greyhound, long nose squashed against the window, hot breath fogging the glass, peered through the window at them. Emily's heart melted. Like most greyhounds he was all smiles and bursting with friendliness.

"Hey, Rock," Bazza called out as he flung open the caravan door. "I brought two cute lady vets to fix you up, mate."

"Don't try and butter us up, Barry. It won't work. And don't get your hopes up, either. We're vets—not magicians. If your dog is lame he could have broken a toe or chipped a bone in his wrist, in which case he won't be racing for months." Emily climbed the step into the van and looked around. "Jesus, kid," she yelped as she took in the mess. "Have you been burgled?" The place looked like a gale force wind had swept through, lifted everything into the air, jumbled them together, and then dropped them willy-nilly throughout the van. She stepped over what looked like a pair of jeans that had recently been used for cleaning up tomato sauce and screwed up her nose.

"Nah, this is normal" said Maggie regarding the clothes piled high on a chair and empty pizza boxes and beer bottles spread across the floor. "It's something you haven't experienced in your 'adults only' bubble. It's called a teenager's room."

The teenager in question, after greeting the excited dog with a hug, glared over his shoulder. "Hey, it's just a caravan. What ya expect?"

"But it's where you *live*," persisted Emily. "*And* where your racing dog lives," she added kicking an empty pizza box out of her way. "How can you expect your greyhound to race at his best when he's stealing stale junk food off the floor? And what about if he wins and gets swabbed by the stewards? God knows what he'd have in his system. Not good enough, Barry." With reluctance she accepted a grungy sneaker presented to her via Rocky's drooling mouth and with two fingers, gingerly placed it on top of the pile of clothes on the chair and tickled the dog behind the ears. "Now, I can't check Rocky in amongst this disgusting mess, so put a lead on your dog and take him outside. I need to return to the car and secure my vet bag."

Damn. She sounded like cranky old Miss Patterson, her eighth grade teacher at St. Judes for Girls. The teacher with no sense of humor and a face like a constipated bulldog. Emily sighed as she left Maggie sitting on a pile of clothes in the middle of a dilapidated sofa inside the van and made her way back to the car.

Was this day ever going to end?

She was tired. She was cranky. And she was scared. What if she'd bitten off more than she could chew with her new mobile vet business?

What if she became the laughing stock of the vet fraternity? First assignment and her client goes and gets himself murdered. She was way over her head with this one. Grabbing the vet bag from the back seat of the car Emily shook her head. Now she sounded like her continually bellyaching mother. Oh God. She'd sworn never to become so negative and depressed that medication was the only way to get through a day. She had nothing to complain about. Not really. After all, she was alive— unlike her client, Craig Benham. Craig had been left sitting on the toilet in a women's restroom, a large bullet hole drilled through his face. Which meant the killer was either a sadistic joker or wanted to not only murder the unfortunate guy, but also humiliate him.

And maybe this sadistic joker was still at large.

Emily let out another sigh. All she wanted to do was swallow a couple of headache pills then stand under a shower and let the hot water ease the aches in her neck and back. And perhaps indulge in a tall glass of something strong, and definitely alcoholic. Maybe then, she'd be her usual optimistic bubbly self.

As she headed back to the caravan, Barry's black and white dog, grinning and wagging his tail, dragged his gangly owner toward her. She eyed the way the dog favored his right front leg. Didn't look too bad. "G'day, Rocky. What have you been up to?"

"Lock on me van door didn't click shut properly and Rocky pushed the door open and ran on the road," Barry growled, rubbing behind the dog's ears with soft fingers. "Idiot dog. Coulda been killed."

As Emily bent to open her bag, the dog's rough tongue slurped along her cheek. "Hey, you can keep your kisses to yourself. Okay?" She rubbed one hand over the top of the dog's head and lightly pulled his ear before hefting him up bodily in her arms and placing him on a wooden picnic table set into the ground with cement. "You should be more careful, Barry. Or better still, you should build a kennel and an outside run for Rocky. It's not healthy for him to be shut inside the van."

"Waste of time if I can't pay me rent and we get tossed out."

After examining and palpitating the dog's right shoulder and leg, Emily dug into her bag for a magnifying glass to check out the pads.

"You're in luck, kid," she said. "No major damage. No toe, wrist, metacarpal, or stopper bone problems, only a little soreness in the pad. Probably picked up grit from the roadway when he went for a run, so if you can hold him still—I'll dig it out."

Barry gripped the dog around the chest while Emily carefully removed several miniscule fragments of grit from the dog's pad, sterilized the wound, and then sprayed it with Centrigen. "Good to go now," she said and lifted the dog down from the table before packing her equipment back in her bag. "When's this race?"

"Saturday at Port Augusta. Reckon Rocky'll be favorite to win too." Barry's fingers reached down and stroked his dog's head. "Rocky and me are going with Dion from the fodder store. He's got a stand at the track on race-days and sells, like, dog leads and kibble and vitamins and stuff. Races a few dogs himself, too."

"Okay, now, listen up," said Emily. "Today's Thursday. You only have two days to get the pad ready to race on. So, I want you to keep it clean and then paint it with several layers of Hard as Nails—that's a lady's nail product which you can purchase at any Chemist." Emily could see Barry focusing on her every word while absently rubbing Rocky's ears. "Paint Hard as Nails on Rocky's pad three times tomorrow and twice on the morning of the race. After that, he should be fine. Just make sure each layer is completely dry before you apply the next."

"I can do that," he declared and then gazed down at his shoes, studying each layer of grime encrusted on the sneakers as though what he saw was more absorbing than the Creation of Man. "And…thanks." Awkward and uncomfortable, he pulled at his studded left ear and dared to meet Emily's eye. "So, like, if there's anything I can do for you while you're here," he continued in a rush. "Just ask. Okay?"

Emily nodded and smiled. Perhaps there was some good in this one after all.

"Well," growled Maggie, coming quietly up behind them. "As a matter of fact, there *is* something you can do for us, Barry."

Both Emily and Barry spun around.

Maggie slammed a large spray paint can onto the wooden picnic table. "You can start by telling us how I found a half-empty red spray paint can hidden underneath your caravan."

"That's not mine!" Barry's face turned white as he stared at the spray can. "I've never seen it before in me life. Honest."

"Okay," drawled Maggie and held up a t-shirt splattered with red paint and with the words GO ROCKY emblazoned across the front. She narrowed her eyes at the glowering teenager. "And I don't suppose *this* belongs to you either…"

18

Someone with an Ulterior Motive

Emily yanked the car door open and growled deep in her throat. Barry Sullivan was dumber than a rock. Maggie had not only found the incriminating can of red spray paint underneath the caravan, she'd also discovered his paint splattered t-shirt right next to it.

Yet still he denied everything.

"What a load of hogwash!" Emily slammed the door shut, jammed the key into the ignition and fired up the motor. And here she was starting to believe there was some good in the little toe-rag. "Huh!" she grunted. "That boy's nothing but a lying, cheating…" She paused. Drew a breath. "*Male!*" she finally spat out. With a last glower at the cause of her fury, she tossed her vet bag onto the back seat and spewed a cloud of dust into the air as she took off.

Both hands on the dash, Maggie gasped and lurched forward. "Calm down, Em, you almost took out a picnic table then. Anger won't cut it as an excuse if you total our landlady's car."

Emily growled again. Of course she was angry. Losing trust in someone was always a huge slap in the face, but after Peter's infidelities her faith in the human male species was way down there along with the cockroaches, rats, blood-sucking lice, and other bottom-licking vermin.

Beside her, Maggie buckled her seat belt and sent one last backward glance over her shoulder at the boy. "Kid's still hugging that damn dog like it's the only friend he's got left in the world."

"And that's only because the stupid dog doesn't know any better."

Maggie laid her head back against the head support and sighed. "You know, even though the kid's as crooked as a busted snake, all I feel is a strange urge to save him from sliding down that slippery slope that'll lead to jail-time."

"All right for you to go all airy-fairy about the little scumbag," said Emily as they bumped toward the open gate of the caravan park. "He tricked me into treating his dog, yet he's been running around town painting cancelled on our posters." She gripped the wheel more tightly. "And who knows what else Barry Sullivan is guilty of?" She blinked and her knuckles showed white against the dark leather of the steering wheel. "Maybe even murder."

"But why?" put in Maggie. "Doesn't make sense. I know Barry wouldn't recognize the truth if he fell head first over it, but why would he kill the track's manager? Why would he want the track to close? Didn't he tell us he'd been offered a part-time job serving in the bar on race days? So why would he help to close the track down before it even opened?"

"One—red paint was used in a series of incidents to sabotage the track. And two—you found a half-empty can of red spray paint under his caravan. What other proof do you need?"

"But he couldn't have painted your windscreen. He was sitting on the steps at our B&B when that took place. Our landlady vouches for him."

"Hmm…there is that." Emily, now heading in the direction of *Emu Bottom Bed and Breakfast*, slowed down for a sleepy-eyed cow that had decided to come into town for a look-see. It was standing in the middle of the road chewing on its cud, probably contemplating why the grass had been replaced by hard black stuff that smelled and tasted like rock. "Well, who do *you* think it is?"

"I've been mulling it over and I reckon our saboteur has to be someone with an ulterior motive. Someone who doesn't want the track to open because it's not in their best interests."

Emily groaned. "Yeah, but who?"

"No idea." Maggie shrugged and shook her head. "Anyway, it's not our problem. We'll be leaving first thing Sunday morning. It's up to the police to investigate Craig's murder and the trouble at the track. Not us."

"But it is. Once that two-bit vandal touched my car it became our problem." Emily stretched her neck to scowl at the loitering cow as she carefully maneuvered her way around the beast. "I want to know who he or she is so I can give them a piece of my mind. Maybe even loosen a tooth or two."

Maggie caught her bottom lip in her teeth and laid a hand on her friend's arm. "Careful my little cock-sparrow," she warned. "One day you'll meet a big bad cat who'll lick his lips, gobble you up, and burp up a feather." She paused. "Like whoever shot Craig Benham."

Emily stared straight ahead. A shiver ran up her spine and it had nothing to do with the weather. The sun, a dominant force in the sky all day had quietly slipped over the horizon but the air had turned clammy. She could see townsfolk ambling along the cobbled main street. No-one seemed in a hurry. After all, hurrying produced rivulets of sweat, caused unquenchable thirst, and stained the armpits of clothes.

She shivered again. Was Craig's murderer out there on the street right now? Mingling with the other unsuspecting townsfolk? Watching their car as she drove along the road? Staring at them? Even smiling? Contemplating another plan to sabotage the track—or them?

With a sigh she shook off the feeling of being watched and concentrated on her next plan of action. Tomorrow they were booked for a second lecture, this time at Kangaroo Downs race-track. Would the secretary, Charles Norton-Phillips, take security more seriously this time? She frowned. Charles was more likely to worry more about the color of his bow tie than security for the track's guest speakers.

If only she knew who to watch out for.

"Oops!" Beside her, Maggie's stomach let out a rumble loud enough to drown out the sound of a passing cattle truck. Maggie giggled. "That's my stomach reminding us that if we hurry we can catch a meal at the pub before the kitchen closes."

Emily rolled her eyes. "Okay, but first I want to make a quick stop at radio station 5RPU."

Maggie groaned. "Why? They don't sell food at the radio station."

"I want to talk to the local DJ. What's his name?"

"Drake Pearson?"

"Yeah, the guy who opened his big mouth and told his listeners that our lectures were cancelled. I want to find out *where* he got that information from and *who* put him up to it." Emily frowned as she searched both sides of the street looking for the 5RPU sign. "Drake Pearson had no right to broadcast those facts without consulting us first."

"Em, you're not thinking straight," Maggie bleated when Emily pulled into a parking space in front of the radio station. "We can't just barge in there like a couple of rednecks."

"We're not barging—we're paying Mr. Drake a visit."

"Why not ring and make an appointment?"

"No, I want to catch this guy before he leaves for the night. I have questions and Drake Pearson has answers."

"What if he's on air? He can't talk to us then."

"He'll talk." Emily flicked the car door closed and marched toward the entrance of the radio station, back ramrod straight, determination in every step. "Even if I have to pull out every one of his damn electric plugs."

"Emily, listen to you." Maggie grabbed at her arm and hung on. "Where's your professionalism? Can't you see you've let Peter's betrayal affect your attitude to everyone else in your life? Don't let my pathetic little brother do this to you."

Emily, the red clouds of anger slowly dissipating as she absorbed Maggie's words, stared at her friend. Maggie was wrong. No way would she allow Peter's cheating sexual exploits affect her attitude to others. She was merely angry because the saboteur had thrown a barb and hooked them neatly into his or her net. Her annoyance had nothing to do with her soon-to-be-ex-husband. Nothing at all. *Poof!* Peter Harrison was merely a back-stabbing, cheating, son-of-a-bitch who…

Emily drew in a deep breath, counted to ten, and let her breath out slowly.

Damn. Maggie was right. She *was* letting Peter's unfaithfulness rule her emotions.

"Thanks, Mags," she said and sent her friend a smile. "What would I do without you?"

"Probably get yourself beat up at least once a week."

Emily laughed and immediately felt the tension in her shoulders and the tightness in her stomach ease—and then disappear. "Maybe, but we *do* need to find out who cancelled our lectures. So…are you with me?"

Maggie nodded then let out a sigh. "Okay, but if this takes longer than ten minutes I can't promise not to rip through the guy's cupboards hunting for anything edible."

19

DJ at Radio 5RPU

Maggie's stomach let out another deafening grumble as she followed Emily through the heavy wooden doorway of 5RPU radio station. She felt her face redden and rubbed her stomach surreptitiously in an attempt to settle it down. No such luck. Only one thing would quieten the rumbles—and it wasn't talking to a local DJ. No, it was sitting down to a juicy steak with salad on the side. Or a plate piled high with spinach and cheese bake. Or chicken parmigiana, ham steak, and hot crispy-on-the-outside and soft-on-the-inside vinegar-soaked fries. Or…

From behind the front desk, a young woman stepped forward. Sun blonde hair pulled back in a thick ponytail, she grinned broadly at her two visitors. "G'day. I'm Stella Turner—receptionist, PA, and general dog's body for Drake Pearson. Welcome to 5RPU, the radio station that reaches every home within a 200k radius of the town from 5am until 10pm seven days a week. We play music, present guest speakers, keep everyone up on local and global news and of course run commercials that will promote your business and reach every listener's home." She rolled her eyes and shrugged, both hands in a don't-blame-me-position. "Sorry, Drake insists I run that spiel past every prospective client who comes through the door. I told him it's more likely to send them running for the hills rather than buy advertising space—but hey, he's the boss. He's the guy who pays me the rent money."

In her early twenties, the blonde was bright-faced and her tanned arms and legs showed she either spent every minute away from work outside in the great outdoors or owned a very large bottle of tanning lotion. "You're the two vet ladies who found Craig Benham draped on the loo, aren't you?"

"Yep," said Maggie. "That's us." Geez, this town's grape vine could lasso and hold the entire city of New York captive.

The receptionist screwed up her nose as though a rotten smell had infiltrated the room. "Sorry," she said and grimaced. "I know I shouldn't speak ill of the dead but like that guy was a creep."

Caught unawares, Maggie glanced across at Emily and blinked. Here was another person bad-mouthing the deceased. "Seems like Craig Benham didn't have much of a fan club around here," Maggie said. "So…what did *you* have against him?"

Stella's nose crinkled in thought. "Like, you know, he was the sort of guy who made your skin go all crawly when he got too close. Know what I mean?"

Emily snorted. "I certainly do."

"Anyway, guess he thought he was Adam to every woman's Eve, but he wasn't. Not even close. Like he had these sweaty hands that he couldn't keep in his pockets. Don't know how many times I had to forcibly remove them from my backside and threaten to tell my boyfriend."

Maggie frowned. "And did you?"

"Nah. Wasn't worth the aggro. The guy was all fake charm on the outside and sneaky like a fox on the inside. Couldn't stand him and he knew it." Stella shook her head, ponytail flying. "One day I saw him kick this stray dog just because the poor dog was lying in the middle of the footpath. And then he went and rang the council and had the dog put down. Said the dog attacked him and it didn't—not even when he stuck the boot in."

"Mongrel," said Emily.

"Probably." The girl frowned. "But that's no reason to kick the poor dog."

"I meant *Benham* not the *dog*," snapped Emily. "Can't abide cruelty to animals."

The girl's sunny smile returned. Her eyes lit up and she leaned forward on the desk. "After all that, what can I do for you ladies today?"

Maggie stepped forward, ready to play nice. "Sorry to bother you without phoning first but—"

"We need to speak to Drake Pearson," Emily butted in. "It's important."

"Sorry, but Drake's on air at the moment."

Emily frowned. "When does he take time off?"

"Time off?" Stella let out a laugh and shook her head so her ponytail bobbed from side to side again. Reminded Maggie of a Barbie doll she'd played dress-ups with as a child. "Drake never takes a rest. He's always on the go. Reckon they should use him in that long-life battery ad on television, you know, instead of the Eveready bunny. Tell you what though, he has a medley of music coming up soon, so he'll have five minutes to spare. Want me to ask if he'll have a quick word with you then?"

Emily opened her mouth to object—probably to inform the receptionist that five minutes was not enough—but with a warning frown, Maggie beat her to it. "Thanks Stella, we'd appreciate that."

Moving out from behind the desk, Stella led them through a swing-door into another room where she indicated a well-upholstered settee in a soft rust color wedged against one wall. "If you could wait here, I'll get Drake to slip out during the next musical selection and have a word. Okay?"

Maggie nodded in agreement then made herself comfortable on the settee. She eyed off a bowl of fruit on a nearby coffee table, sighed when she discovered the apples and bananas were plastic, and settled down to wait. But not Emily. Unable to sit still, Emily began her usual pacing. Up and down. Up and down. Made Maggie bone weary just watching her.

To take her mind off food, Maggie studied the room. She could see the red ON AIR lights blinking over a door to the right of the settee and a small kitchenette to the left. Although only a small area, every available space was utilized. Iridescent yellow plaster showed through the gaps on the walls which were covered with photos and posters of local events—an agricultural show, cattle milling around the sale yards, a parade marching down the main street, a faded black and white photo of the Kangaroo Downs pub depicting life in the early 1900's and even a picture of the B&B where they were currently staying, back when it had been a local church. Maggie noticed several black robed nuns posing out the front and wondered which one was the persistent ghost who refused to join her maker.

Finally, Stella poked her head through the doorway, all smiles. "Drake will see you now. But remember, he only has five minutes."

Maggie could see Emily ready to object again so nudged her to be quiet. "That's fine," she said to the bubbly receptionist. "We really only have one question to ask him."

"One?" objected Emily.

"Think about it."

Emily blinked and then smiled and Maggie could see the understanding in her friend's eyes. Of course they only had one question to ask.

So when Drake Pearson, with his immature goatee and purple and green hair appeared through the doorway, Emily leapt out in front of him and wasted no time in putting that question to him. "Who the hell gave you permission to inform everyone in a 200k radius that our lectures for today and tomorrow had been cancelled?"

Drake's welcoming smile slowly melted. He blinked at Emily. "Come again?"

"You heard me."

Dressed in jeans so tight they looked like they'd been sprayed on with black paint and an equally tight psychedelic shirt that would have made a rainbow appear drab, the DJ gave Emily a big-eyed, open-mouthed stare that definitely said *we have a psycho loose in town,* and took a large step backwards.

Time to intervene.

Pushing past Emily, Maggie grabbed the bewildered man's hand and pumped it three times, hanging on a little longer than necessary to prevent him from bolting into the safety of his studio. "Hi Drake," she said. "Please forgive my friend. She's a little upset about what's been happening since we arrived in this town. I'm Maggie Post and this is Emily Harrison. We're the vets who were engaged to give lectures on Equine Management at the church hall this afternoon. No one turned up because you told them, on air, that our lectures had been cancelled. In other words, your message caused our workshop to be a non-event."

"Aaha." Drake snapped out of his confusion and his eyes lit up with professional thirst. "So, you're the two vet ladies who found—"

"Yes, yes," broke in Emily, determined not to be distracted. "We found Craig Benham's body in Joe and Jean's restrooms. Or to be more precise, Maggie found him and I later verified he was dead. However, that's not the reason we're here. What we want is the name of the person who advised you to cancel our lecture. If we can find out the perpetrator of *that* scam—we'll have the identity of the saboteur."

Drake slid his headphones over his ears, listened intently for a couple of seconds then slid them back down around his neck again. "Actually, Chief Constable Kelly has already asked me that question."

Maggie turned this information over in her head. So, Constable Kelly had already been here? Hmm…that was quick thinking on his part.

Drake shook his head. "And I'm afraid I have to give you the same answer I gave him. I don't know who left the memo on my desk."

Emily glowered at him. "How could you not know? Surely you'd see someone putting a note on your desk."

"Hey, lady, I'm not around 24/7. I *do* take meal and toilet breaks. In fact, I found that memo when I came back from buying a coffee and a vanilla slice from the café next door… around four o'clock this afternoon.

"And you don't know who put it there?"

He shook his head. "Sorry. I normally have a pile of memos and adverts sitting beside the microphone to announce throughout the broadcast. Some Stella puts there, some come in over the phone and I scribble them down, others are left on my desk by people dropping in. Anyway, as soon as I saw this note about the lectures being cancelled I read it out over the air."

"What did the note look like?"

Drake gave Emily an eye roll. "Like any other note, I guess."

"Describe it."

With one eye fixed warily on Emily, Drake rubbed a finger along the side of his nose. "Hmm…let's see. It was printed on a scrap of paper torn from another message in the pile—an advert for bathroom supplies, I think." He gave a one-shouldered shrug. "Anyway, I thought the chief constable left the note while Stella and I were in the café…you know, cancelling the lectures because of Craig's murder." He took another step back. "An honest assumption."

"But you must have some idea who had access to the radio station while you were out," Emily persisted.

Drake shook his head. "Lady, it could have been anyone. Lots of people drop in here. Delivery guys, sponsors, cleaners, tourists. Any one off the street has access to the studio." He gestured with both hands. "It's not Fort Knox you know. As long as no one barges into the studio while I'm broadcasting, it's pretty much open house." Hand on the door he smiled apologetically. "And talking of broadcasting—song's almost finished so that's my cue to get back to work. But hey, I'll put a message over the air, A.S.A.P, that your lectures will go ahead as planned at the race track tomorrow. Okay?"

Seemed like that was all they were going to pry out of Drake Pearson. Maggie sighed. It wasn't the DJ's fault today's lecture was cancelled. He was merely the go-between. "Thanks for your help, Drake," she said. "If we need to talk further, we know where to find you."

Once Drake disappeared inside his private booth to continue with the evening broadcast, Emily turned to Maggie and pulled a face. "None the wiser, are we?"

"Nope." Maggie snagged a paper cup from beside the water dispenser and helped herself to a drink.

"Let's go ask young Stella out there a few more questions. See if she's more observant than head-in-his-earphones, Drake Pearson."

Feeling a little more optimistic, Maggie downed the last of her water in one quick swig and followed Emily into the reception area. "Stella's gone," she said peering at the empty desk.

"And she hasn't even bothered to lock the door after her."

"Of course she hasn't." Maggie let out a laugh. "It's different in small country towns. No-one bothers to lock up or worry about leaving their keys in the car. It's a more casual and neighborly life style."

"Perhaps they *should* worry," Emily said. "After all, there's a sadistic saboteur on the loose."

"Yes," Maggie said and stared at a photo on the wall behind Stella's desk. A photo of a baby bull calf crying out for its mother which was *almost* enough to convert her to vegetarianism. "*And* a callous murderer," she added. "Whoever shot Craig Benham is one of their own."

20

The Saboteur Strikes Again

After a delicious meal at the pub, where they'd made the cut by exactly seven-and-a-half minutes, Maggie's stomach was finally placated. Especially after that decadent desert of mouth-watering pavlova heaped high with colorful slices of fruit and cream, so thick, the spoon stood up like a sentinel at the gate. Naturally, it would have been impolite to refuse a second helping.

As Maggie and Emily entered the hallway of the B&B, their landlady, Lola Brigetta, sailed toward them like a large colorful yacht. The fact she was dressed in a loose flowing Muumuu of brilliant Hawaiian pinks and yellows only added to the image.

She smiled and raised her eyebrows at them. "Would you ladies care for a nightcap?"

Maggie eyed the half full whisky bottle clutched in Lola's be-ringed fingers and grinned in appreciation. "Aha…how could we say no to Johnny Walker? You have excellent taste, Lola."

Lola's smile set her eyes alight and she let out a deep belly laugh. "Come join me on the balcony. I'm dying to hear about your day." Lola led them through the stately lounge room and from there to a set of double glass doors which led onto a small and intimate balcony. "You might need to use a hefty spray of *Buzz Off* to deter the hungry dragons masquerading as mosquitoes, but there's a breeze outside. Makes the heat more tolerable."

Maggie threw herself into a canvas deck chair at the left of a small green metal table and kicked off her shoes. Ah, this was the way to end a day. She glanced across at Emily, who, instead of her usual restless pacing, lowered herself into a red and white striped canvas chair and sighed. Her best friend looked exhausted. And no wonder. This was the first assignment for Emily's new venture, *Vets2U*, and it had disaster written all over it.

"While the highlight of *my* day has been painting the attic midnight black with a sprinkling of emerald stars, I can't wait to hear what you two to have been up to," said Lola selecting three glasses from an antique wooden drinks' cabinet tucked into the corner of the balcony and pouring an inch of whisky into each glass. "The mystery you lovely ladies have generated since driving into town is more exciting than the latest Sue Grafton novel."

Emily took the proffered glass and shook her head. "Can't say the excitement has been much fun for us though."

Lola banged the heel of her hand into her forehead. "Sorry, I'm always sticking my big foot in my even bigger mouth. Of course it's been a lousy day for you two. So, what can I do to make it better?"

"For a start you can sit down and enjoy the elixir of life with us." Maggie smiled and held her glass of whisky in the air. "To friendship," she said and deepened her smile. Lola was fun to be around. Bubbly and overflowing with joy and life. She'd even stuck up for that little toe-rag, Bazza, because she knew he wasn't guilty of sabotaging Emily's car. The sort of person you'd be proud to call your friend. "You know," Maggie said puffing out her chest, "I'm rather honored to be likened to a Sue Grafton novel."

"Thank you." Lola smiled at Maggie and sat down. "By the way, did you find out who cancelled your workshops?"

"Nah. Struck out there." Emily swirled her glass and watched the liquid slosh around inside the glass. "We did question Drake Pearson but he couldn't give us any answers. Evidently it's open house down at the radio station. No locks, no security videos and an invitation to drop in whenever you like. Anyone could have waltzed in off the street and left the message on Drake's desk." Emily cradled her glass until the liquid stilled and then stared at the contents. "But at least Drake promised to let everyone know the whole cancellation drama was a hoax so we should get an audience tomorrow."

Maggie watched tension tighten her friend's forehead and reached across to touch Emily on the arm. "Em, if you're going to be at the top of your form tomorrow, down your drink, sit back in your chair and relax. Let Johnny Walker do his job."

"I agree," said Lola. "So…down the hatch, ladies." Lola upended her glass and emptied it in one swig. "Here, I'll turn the radio on low so we can settle back and listen to some light music while we finish off the bottle. Feel free to use the bug spray if the mozzies threaten to carry you away."

"Sounds good to me," said Maggie and clicked glasses with Emily then followed Lola's example by tossing back her drink in one go.

She closed her eyes. The breeze, so light it barely moved the leaves on the large peppercorn tree which provided shade for the balcony during the day, brushed her hot cheeks. The only sound came from the soft music on the radio and a family of grasshoppers who made *brrpt* noises as they danced and played in the grass. Ah, the peace of country life beat the constant noise of the city any day.

She heard Emily telling Lola about their run-in with Charles Norton-Phillips, the secretary of the race-track. Emily couldn't believe a man too up himself to help set up chairs in the hall could be a successful Real Estate manager with the know-how and commitment to the long hours needed to make a go of a company scattered over such a large area. Lola agreed. Said he was a pompous idiot who fell into the job when his father, who owned four of the six Real Estate buildings from Port Pirie through to Port Lincoln, ended up in a nursing home after a bad car crash. Things at each agency quickly deteriorated when Charles took the reins. Last she'd heard he'd sacked eight of the eighteen employees and demanded the ten remaining workers carry the entire load while he strutted around the countryside like royalty. Where he got the money from for his fast cars and the recent renovations to his house, she didn't know. The real estate business wasn't thriving in the current economy.

It was when Aerosmith's Steve Tyler came to the end of AC/DC's 'You Shook Me All Night Long' and the voice of the DJ informed listeners that Kangaroo Downs Fodder store had a sale of hay nets on that Maggie opened her eyes. Three hay nets for ten dollars. And if you bought more than thirty dollars' worth there'd be a free bale of hay thrown in.

Maggie roused herself to listen. Not that she was interested in buying more hay nets. Her two horses weren't stabled and Alex, her daughter's horse, already owned a dozen in every color of the rainbow. No, it was the voice that drew her attention. She leaned forward and frowned. "That doesn't sound like Drake Pearson on the radio."

"No, it isn't." Lola swirled the whisky around in her glass. "Drake has a few wannabe DJ's at his beck and call and usually lets them do a quick stint between nine and midnight." She took a small sip of her drink, savoring it on her tongue. "That's John Taylor, nicknamed Ape. Jack of all trades and master of none. Helps out on farms at hay-stacking time or at the diner when Jean needs muscles. Late-twenties. Hair looks like he's either seen a ghost or he plugs himself into the electricity circuit on getting out of bed each morning. *Me,* I wouldn't trust him as far as I could boot him while wearing flip-flops, but evidently he's the keenest of all the wannabee radio-jocks so he's on air most nights."

Maggie frowned as the first beats of Justin Bieber's, *As Long as You Love Me* blared from the radio. "You mean, Hairy Guy?"

"Yep, that's the one." Lola let out a giggle that made her sound more like a high school kid than a middle-aged landlady. "That's how he got his nickname. He'd make an ideal cast member for Planet of the Apes."

"Isn't he Barry Sullivan's mate?"

"Mmm." Lola pulled a face. "More's the pity. Quite a bit older than

Barry and a bad influence on the youngster. I've always suspected that whenever Barry's in trouble, it's Ape who made the bullets and talked Barry into firing them."

The song came to an abrupt halt and was immediately replaced by John Taylor's deep growling voice. "I have an important newsflash, folks," he said. "Mr. Joseph Bartolli, who was in custody for the murder of local man, Craig Benham, has been set free." Maggie pictured the guy's eyes narrowing as he made the announcement. There was no love lost between him and Joe. "We've been informed by the police that Mr. Bartolli's alibi for the time of the deceased's murder has been verified. Mr. Bartolli has witnesses who can verify he was travelling to Port Augusta to pick up a large meat order yesterday morning when the victim was killed."

"Aaah," said Lola.

"Hmm," said Maggie.

"Right," said Emily with a deep sigh. "I guess that means the police are back where they started from—a dead body and no suspects."

*****

An hour later, drooping with fatigue, Maggie followed Emily up the stairs, one leaden foot after the other. It had been a big day and it wasn't finished yet. They still had to feed Jackson and settle him down for the night.

Resisting the urge to collapse on the bed, Maggie bent and tickled the tiny Macropod under the chin. "Hang on, baby boy. Supper will be ready in a few minutes." She collected a bottle, teat, spoon, and the can of joey milk to make up his night feed. "You're a lucky boy," she told him, smiling at the adorable expression on his face. "You'll be off to the wildlife center in the morning and have lots of baby joeys to play with."

Emily lifted Jackson carefully from his comfortable nest and snuggled him close to her body, rocking him like a baby. "I swear you've grown a quarter of an inch since we found you this morning," she said, lightly running a finger over one tiny ear and down his furry head. "What do you think, Mags?"

"Oh, definitely," teased Maggie, lifting the bottle out of the saucepan of hot water and shaking it. "Master Jackson Kangaroo will soon be so big and fat he'll burst out of his fur."

Emily shook her head and tutted. "Don't listen to her, baby. Just put your paws over your ears. Aunty Maggie doesn't mean it."

"Okay, all ready." Maggie sat on the bed, bottle in one hand and her other outstretched to take Jackson from Emily. "Look what I've got for you, Jackson. Yum! Yum! Just don't expect me to sing any lullabies to get you to sleep, okay?" She shook her head. "Anyway, I've forgotten the words to Christopher Robin."

Emily laughed. "Christopher Robin? I remember you singing that song to Judy."

"Don't remind me." Maggie waited for the joey to wrap his mouth around the rubber teat and within seconds he started to suck. She smiled down at him, her smile widening when his eyes, dreamy and blissed out fastened on her face. All babies had that special magnetism, a combination of smell and pheromones that made you want to cuddle them and protect them.

Emily let out a laugh as she put away the can of Woomeroo and then wiped the cupboard down with a damp rag. "Where have those twelve years gone?" she said. "I remember the day you brought Judy home from hospital. She wasn't much bigger than little Jackson here and I couldn't get over how tiny her finger nails were."

"Have a look at these nails," said Maggie holding up one of Jackson's tiny paws. "If his claws are anything to go by this little guy will end up a very large male buck."

Ten minutes later, after Jackson was fed and settled into his bed, Maggie dragged her suitcase from the corner of the room and dug around inside until she found her iridescent pink night-dress. She watched Emily slide into bed, wriggle a couple of times and then drag the sheet up around her neck. "Comfortable?"

"Ooh, yes. This bed is heaven." Emily almost purred. "Hope I can sleep, though. I always have trouble getting off to sleep in a strange bed."

"Me too. That's why I always bring my own pillows."

By the time Maggie returned from the bathroom and climbed into bed, Emily was snoring. She must have gone to sleep the moment her blonde head hit the pillow. Not so Maggie. While downstairs she'd been relaxed and sleepy, now she was wide awake. Her two duck-down pillows, always soft at home, suddenly grew hard lumps and no matter how much she tossed and turned she couldn't get comfortable on the unfamiliar bed.

Did the room have a strange odor to it or was the smell coming from outside and drifting through the open window? Nose alert, she sniffed again. A sort-of mixture between a dumpster and something that smelled like musty dead bodies.

Nah…that couldn't be right.

From the corner of her eye she caught what she thought was a flash of movement but when she narrowed her eyes and peered through the darkness there was nothing there. And was that a soft knocking sound coming from behind the walls? She strained her ears to hear more but suddenly the room was quiet as the grave. Oh God, no, not the image she was looking for.

In desperation, Maggie snuggled deeper into the mattress. Geez she was letting her imagination get the better of her. Of course it wasn't the ghostly nun. So what if the poor woman died in this room? Lola probably told this story to all her guests merely to promote her B&B. Ghosts didn't exist. It was all bunkum. And even if a stray nun *did* decide she wasn't ready to party in Heaven and figured she'd hang around her old church in ghostly form, she'd be sweet and kind and loving, definitely not scary. Right?

Maggie snatched the sheet up over her head, cemented her eyelids closed and curled into a fetal ball. Perhaps it would help if she tried meditating—or counting sheep—or maybe even humming lullabies. Hey, her mind was too active—that's all. It wasn't every day a person was unlucky enough to come across a dead body while minding her own business in the privacy of a public restroom.

And what about the comedy of errors at their cancelled lecture this afternoon? And the fact their car had been sabotaged? And the situation with Barry? Which reminded her she needed to confront the boy, find out if he was telling the truth about the red paint. First thing in the morning she'd go for a walk to the caravan park and sort him out. And on the way back she'd check at the garage to see if they'd finished replacing the windscreen and the four wheels on Emily's Echo.

It was hot and stifling with the sheet over her head so Maggie eased the sheet down, stretched out into a more comfortable position and forced her body to relax. She counted baby lambs springing playfully over a fat old ewe. This ploy must have worked because the ewe metamorphosed into Lola's legendary ghostly nun…Sister Ursula. Well, that's who she said she was in the dream.

Ursula, dressed in long black robes, her empty eye sockets staring unseeing at Maggie, leaned over the bed. Her fingers, cold bony claws, grasped the top of Maggie's arm and dug in deep like some unearthly creature holding its prey before devouring it.

"Thou shalt not kill!" Ursula told Maggie in a thunderous voice that would have gone down well in a church full of sinners. "Thou shalt not covet thy neighbor's wife!"

"Erk…" Bile caught in Maggie's throat. She could feel blood draining from her face while her heart crashed around in her chest. Thinking she was going to die, she squeezed her eyes closed and held her breath.

Ursula began knocking her skeletal fist on the bed's headboard inches from her head. The knocking grew louder and louder and came closer and closer. Maggie screamed.

"Maggie! Maggie! Wake up! You're having a bad dream. You've been yelling commandments in a voice loud enough to curdle milk and now you've woken Lola. Sounds like she's banging on our door with a rolling pin."

Heart still thumping, Maggie sat up so quickly Emily's face swam in her vision, while Ursula, now floating in the air, stabbed a long bony finger in her direction then growled deep in her non-existent throat and disappeared. "Oh, my God! She's real!" Maggie clutched her friend for support.

Emily poured water from a jug on the bedside table into a glass and handed it to Maggie. "Here, drink this and calm down while I open the door."

"It wasn't me quoting from the commandments," whispered Maggie clutching the glass like a lifebuoy in a storm. "*She* was here. *She* was beside my bed."

"Who?"

"Ursula."

"Maggie, you're not making sense. Ursula who?"

"You know…the dead nun. The nun who won't leave this earthly plane. She was in the room and she was warning me about not killing and not coveting my neighbor's wife."

"Come on, Mags, have a sip of water and calm down. You were dreaming. It was you calling out in a weird voice." She gave a stiff smile. "Almost made me swallow my tonsils in fright."

Maggie swung her legs over the side of the bed, placed the glass back on the bedside table and stood up. "No, it was Ursula." She glanced around the room, now lit by the 60watt globe hanging from the ceiling. She almost expected the nun to walk through the nearest wall and introduce herself to Emily. "Em, why would the ghost visit *me*? What was she trying to tell me by quoting from the bible? Was it a clue?"

The knocking on the door grew louder. "Let us in!" It was Lola.

Emily shook her head. "No, Mags, it was a nightmare. Probably that extra slice of pavlova you couldn't refuse for desert." She unlocked the door and took a step back as Lola and a strange man dressed in khaki shorts and shirt with the Wildlife Rescue logo on the pocket barreled through the doorway. The man cradled Mephistopheles, Lola's big orange cat, in his arms.

And the cat was covered in blood.

21

Another Suspect

Emily, eyes on the blood-soaked cat, gasped and felt a shiver run down her back. "Oh, my God! What happened?"

"Sorry to bust in on you like this, ladies," said the man in khaki, looking everywhere but at the two half-dressed women. "I'm Jimmy Black from the wildlife center. I know it's early, but I was passing through, just picked up a sick possum from nearby, so I thought I'd drop in and take the orphaned joey off your hands." He looked down at the limp cat in his arms. "Couldn't believe my eyes when I found this poor critter on the doorstep. Thought he was dead."

"It's Mephistopheles!" broke in Lola, her face ashen, her voice almost a squeak. "Can you fix him? Please!"

"Jesus!" Emily moved closer, her eyes raking over the big orange cat, her fingers touching him ever so gently. Her stomach did a back flip as she studied his wounds and she couldn't contain the gasp of anger that sprang from her lips. A crushing, fierce anger that sent the blood in her temples pounding and her nails digging into the palms of both hands. The cat had blood oozing from multiple stab wounds in its stomach and neck and its back legs were tied together with thick twine.

Who did this barbaric deed?

Gently, Emily took the cat from the man's arms, the metallic smell of blood almost making her gag. She laid him carefully on the bed.

Only a monster could do this to an innocent animal.

She felt for a pulse. Thank God. Mephistopheles was still alive, but his pulse was weak and thready. Lola's giant stray must be made of stronger DNA than the normal pampered feline to survive such a brutal attack. And when she gently cut the twine holding his back legs together, the cat's eyes fluttered open. Bewildered, pain-filled eyes. Eyes that seemed to ask her why—what had he ever done to deserve this unholy punishment?

There was a growl from beside her and Emily turned to see Maggie with their vet bag open and a syringe at the ready. Face set in a grimace and eyes narrowed, Maggie looked angry enough to eat rocks as she bent to swab a patch of the cat's fur. "First up, I'll give him a painkiller," she said.

"Okay," agreed Emily. "And then, if we're going to save this poor fellow's life, one of us will have to take him to the local vet, pronto. There's nothing in our bag that will do more than keep him alive until he has access to surgery."

Maggie nodded but before she could open her mouth to speak, Lola, like something from a horror movie, lumbered across the room. Head covered in large pink and blue hair rollers, face eerie and otherworldly under a thick green facial mask, she took one look at the mutilated cat, limp on the bed, and let out a curse loud enough to wake every ghost in the old church.

"He's going to die, isn't he?" she howled as Maggie sent a shot of morphine into the cat's system.

Emily put an arm around Lola's shoulder and gently led her toward the door. "Lola, calm down. I want you to ring the town's vet and tell him we have an emergency. Tell him I'll meet him at his surgery in five minutes with the patient. And make sure he realizes it *is* an emergency."

"But-but who—"

"At this stage *who* doesn't matter." Although later, when she *did* find the culprit—he or she would likely be seeking emergency treatment themselves. Pushing these thoughts from her mind as a distraction, Emily placed an oxygen mask over the cat's mouth. "With the blood

Mephistopheles has already lost—if he isn't attended to within the next fifteen, twenty minutes—we'll lose him. Now, go!"

"Of course. Leave it to me." Lola hastily finished knotting the ties on her flimsy, see-through dressing gown and hurried toward the door. "I just can't understand it," she muttered as she brushed past Jimmy Black. "Why would anyone want to hurt poor old Mephistopheles? No wonder he didn't come when I called him last night. Thought maybe he'd found himself a girlfriend."

Jimmy Black who'd already lifted Jackson from his nest of jumpers, stood at the door, the joey cuddled in his arms. He shook his head. "I'd like five minutes with the mongrel who did that to Lola's cat. Just five minutes. Never seen anything like it—not even out in the wild."

"Seems to me the saboteur is mighty determined to scare us into going home," put in Maggie.

Emily struggled to control her rising anger as she put a stethoscope to the cat's chest. "Well, he's failed. What this thug has done to Mephistopheles has made me more determined to find him, report him to the police and see him rot in jail."

Lola hurried back into the room, one hand hooked under the handle of Mephistopheles's carry-cage. "Dr. Ashford is five minutes away from his surgery," she informed them and then shooed Jimmy Black out, telling him the ladies needed to get dressed.

"Good." By now Emily was too concerned with the cat's weakening pulse rate to give the matter of the saboteur more thought. "And Lola, okay if I borrow your car?"

"Keys are on the kitchen table. Vet surgery is the last building to the right on Main Street. And please, ring me the moment you and Dr. Ashford have any news. No expense spared in treating him. Okay? Mephistopheles might be a scruffy stray—but he's *my* scruffy stray." As she watched Emily throw on some clothes and then carry the cat through the doorway, Lola's face crumpled and she wiped at her eyes with the back of one hand. "That's if the poor little bugger makes it."

*****

When Emily rushed through the clinic doorway with Mephistopheles sprawled unmoving in his cage, she was pleased to discover a dedicated surgery with modern instruments, a treatment area, and a brightly decorated consulting room. For a country vet, Dr. David Ashford's rooms were spotless and surprisingly well equipped. Which meant the tall, gaunt faced, forty-something vet who greeted her, either came into the practice with a very healthy bank account—or he'd been working twenty-hour days, seven days a week to set it up.

"You were lucky to catch me near the surgery," he told Emily as he examined the patient. "Lola rang when I was two minutes away. I was coming back from a hellishly complicated foaling sixty miles north of town. Any earlier and I wouldn't have made it in time."

This was the man Maggie and she would be working with at the track on Saturday. Emily studied Dr. David Ashford more closely. He didn't sport a 6 0'clock shadow—more like a five-day old forest. Dark untamed hair, badly in need of a brush and a cut, curled on the collar of his olive green polo shirt. Emily smiled to herself. The Kangaroo Downs vet reminded her of one of her favorite girlhood literary characters, Heathcliff, from 'Wuthering Heights'. She almost expected the dark-haired vet to stare at her, eyes bleak and brooding and growl: *'I have not broken your heart—you have broken it: and in breaking it, you have broken mine'*.

Fatigue showed in every line of the man's body, from his drooping shoulders and tired red rimmed eyes to the shuffle of his feet. He looked like he often forgot to eat. Worrying that he may not be up to performing the intricate surgery needed to save the cat, Emily offered her services, explaining that she was a fully qualified vet who had only recently given up her own veterinary practice in the city and now was a member of a two-woman team, *Vets2U*.

"Offer accepted," he said and grinned. A grin that pushed through the exhaustion and lit up his dark face. "With two snatched fifteen-minute naps over the last forty-eight hours I'm more than happy for you to assist me. In fact, if I had the energy, I'd be on my bended knees thanking you." He injected a needle connected to an IV containing anesthetic into a vein in the cat's front leg, then rubbed his hands together and straightened his shoulders. "Now, Emily—okay to call you Emily?"

"Only if I can call you David."

He nodded and reached for a set of serrated forceps in readiness to clamp off blood vessels. "Right—Emily—let's see if we can do a Humpty Dumpty act and put poor old Mephistopheles back together again, shall we?"

The operation proved long and complicated. With so many abdominal stab wounds, they were forced to perform three-layer closures. The first, suturing the body wall, the second, stitching the connective tissue between the body wall and skin, and finally, the skin closure.

At last Emily was able to settle the still-sedated cat on a bed of shredded paper inside a hospital cage to recuperate. They'd done all they could—now it was all up to the giant cat's tough moggy genes.

With a groan, Emily stretched the kinks from her back and turned to face her fellow vet. "You know, I can't understand why people in this town don't lock their doors and windows. Seems a logical procedure to me.

David laughed. "Kangaroo Downs is a country town and I guess everyone knows everyone else, trusts them, and doesn't think it necessary to lock doors like you do in the big bad city."

"Well, one of your *trusted* townsfolk had a go at killing Mephistopheles either during the night or in the early hours of this morning and left him on the doorstep of the B&B for us to find," she reminded him. "In my opinion—that's *not* someone you can trust."

"You're right. Of course. Whoever performed those horrific injuries on Lola's cat is mentally disturbed."

"Mentally disturbed? Hell, more like the Devil Incarnate. And what about Craig Benham? Seems like one of your *trusted* townspeople shot off Craig's face and left him in a restroom at Joe's diner. Probably the same 'mentally disturbed' person who took a knife to Mephistopheles."

Dr. David Ashton pushed a stray lock of his dark untidy hair away from his eyes and studied the blood smeared scalpel in his hand before immersing it in a bowl of hospital-grade disinfectant. "Sorry, but I have more sympathy for the cat than I do for Benham."

Emily glanced up from scrubbing the metal operating table and frowned at the ill-masked venom in David's voice. Until now, the man she'd been working with had seemed gentle, harmless, kind. So it came as a shock to hear the hatred and see the abhorrence emanating from him. Obviously there was bad history between David and the murdered man. "You didn't like Benham?" she asked softly.

David's voice turned harsh and his movements jerky as he continued scouring the surgical instruments they'd used during the operation. "You could say that. In fact, Benham is the only person I've ever hated."

Emily frowned but continued to scrub. "Seems like the victim had very few admirers in this town—which makes finding his killer akin to locating a needle in the proverbial haystack."

Maybe it was the quiet and otherworldliness of very early morning or the familiarity of working together, but next thing David Ashton's abrasive voice cut through the air like the hammering of a nail.

"Craig Benham killed my wife."

Jesus! Emily dropped the scrubbing brush and fastened her full attention on her colleague. Peaceful country town? Kangaroo Downs was more like one of those angst-ridden towns you see in television's long-running series, *Midsomer Murders.*

"My wife constantly needed reassurance." David spoke without looking up, his voice so quiet Emily had to lean closer to hear him. "Right from the time I first met Steph I knew she was fragile. But when we married and came here, I was busy setting up the vet practice and Steph was home alone far too much. If I'd been there for her, my beautiful, vulnerable wife wouldn't have strayed into that monster's arms." With dark haunted eyes, David focused his inner anger on cleaning the surgical equipment. "Craig Benham promised Steph the world and then betrayed her. Captivated her. Used sex and charm as a tool until he'd talked her into transferring our money into his bank account and then he tossed her aside like a wet paper bag. Laughed in her face when she told him she loved him." Actions jerky, David continued to scour the same pair of forceps over and over again—like the contaminated instrument was Craig Benham's unclean soul.

Phew! Emily chewed on her bottom lip. This was more than she'd bargained for when she'd offered to assist the dark haired, wild, Heathcliff look-alike during the cat's operation. "David, I *do* know where you're coming from," she said, mind on another cheating individual who had recently betrayed her. "But you can't blame yourself."

It was like he wasn't listening. Instead, he seemed to be reliving the tragic events all over again in his head. "Steph had been off her depression tablets for a month prior to her death. I guess she thought she didn't need them while she had a man telling her every day how gorgeous and sexy she was. So, when Benham threw her out, told her she was a tramp and he never wanted to see her again, she couldn't accept the rejection. She came home, wrote me a note—which I didn't find until the following day because once again, I was away at a vet's conference—climbed into her car, and drove over the nearest cliff."

Holy Toledo! This man had every reason to hate Craig Benham.

In fact, he had every reason to kill him.

22

A Disturbing Encounter

Maggie sipped her coffee and listened to Lola retell the story for the third time of how Mephistopheles had chosen her for his new owner. How he'd walked in when she'd opened the door one morning, strutted into the lounge room, jumped up on her most comfortable chair, turned around three times then curled up and gone to sleep, purring all the while.

She was getting ready to pat Lola on the arm and tell her also for the third time that Mephistopheles was a very perceptive cat to choose her when the discordant sound of the phone broke into their conversation.

Lola almost tipped the chair over in her haste to grab the hands-free from the table. "Emily?"

Maggie watched the older woman's face sag and then crease into a frown. "Oh. I see. No, I was expecting a phone call from the vet. Well, yes, I *do* have a vacancy—but have you checked your watch recently? It's five o'clock in the morning."

Ear squashed hard against the white plastic, Lola whooshed another sigh. "Fair enough. I'll have a room ready for you and your wife in half an hour, but please, in future, try to book in advance."

After ending the conversation, Lola turned to Maggie with a shrug. "A couple passing through on their way to Adelaide. Need somewhere to sleep during the day as it's cooler driving at night." She put the chewed cigarette back in the pocket of her see-through wrap and put a hand on Maggie's shoulder. "I'd better make up the bed in room 15."

Maggie squeezed Lola's hand then pushed back her chair and collected the empty coffee cups ready to stack in the dishwasher. "Anything you'd like me to do to help?"

"No, it's only a matter of putting clean sheets on the bed and making sure everything's ship-shape. Why don't you go back to bed and catch up on lost sleep? I'll wake you in two or three hours when I've rustled up some breakfast."

An icy shiver shimmered down Maggie's spine at the very thought of returning to her room. "Not likely." She rolled her eyes at Lola. "Not with your resident ghost pointing her skeletal finger and blaming me for every sin in the Bible."

Lola shook her head as she walked toward the kitchen door. "You were having a nightmare, sweetie. Must have been the booze and my talk of ghosts and—"

"Ursula was no dream."

Lola stopped dead in her tracks and spun around, eyes wide. "How do you know the nun's name?" Her voice was barely above a whisper. "I didn't tell you."

"Believe me when I say Ursula is quite capable of introducing herself. If that's all she did it wouldn't be so bad, but when she started spouting scary stuff from the bible—"

"Ursula *spoke* to you?"

"Couldn't shut her up."

It was tricky to see through the thickness of the green beauty gunk on Lola's face but the bits Maggie could see had gone the color of milk. "Did I tell you that when Ursula speaks it means someone is going to die?"

"What?" Maggie felt her mouth drop open and her heart rate double. "No, Lola, you did *not* share that gruesome piece of information with me." She grabbed a breath and pressed one hand on her racing heart. "Are you saying…because your stupid ghost spoke to me…I'm now going to die?"

"No, no. It's just a story. A sort of legend. You know, a piece of oral history that came with the church. No need to worry," said Lola, hands in the air in the traditional 'it's okay' position. "And it's not the person Ursula speaks to who's going to die." She shrugged. "Just a general prediction of death."

"Hmm…maybe she's a bit late finding out about Craig Benham."

"You could be right," said Lola, unease creasing the green skin between her eyes. "Anyway, I'd better get room 15 ready for the Burtons or they'll be sleeping on a bare mattress."

"If you need a hand, just give me a yell. And don't forget to clean that green junk off your face before you open the door to the Burtons or they'll run screaming for the hills."

Maggie shook off her own apprehension as she watched Lola sail out of the kitchen. No way could she go back to sleep now knowing the ghostly nun was camped in her room, eager to pass on more messages of doom and death. Instead, she'd shower and change and maybe go for a stroll down to the caravan park.

If she was going to help Emily with this investigation there was a certain young lad with multiple piercings and a bad attitude who knew more than he was letting on. And early morning, before the sun came up, might just be a good time to offer him food and convince him to start talking.

*****

A BRIBE: an inducement, a payoff, a carrot.

After transferring the last mini-packet of potato chips and a miniscule bag of peanuts from the goodie-bowl on the coffee table in their room to her shoulder bag, Maggie let out a growl. Damn. Her 'carrot' wasn't anywhere near large enough to satisfy her prey.

Like huntresses of old, Maggie gathered her wits about her and set off to track down more food.

Lacking a bow and arrow, she set off along the main street in search of an open shop—preferably one that sold already-prepared food—only to discover all doors firmly shut. Damn. Perhaps 5.30am wasn't the ideal time to visit Barry after all. Almost ready to abandon the chase and tackle her quarry later in the day, Maggie noticed a thin strip of light shining under the door of BAKELICIOUS, the town's only bakery. Aha. Drawn to the light like a kid to chocolate, Maggie quickened her pace. Of course. Why hadn't she thought of that? All bakers started baking at an ungodly hour every day of the week.

"Sorry to bother you," she said to the large red-faced man who opened the door. Dressed in a thick white coat and cook's hat it was no wonder his face was red. She wanted to ask him why he didn't do the baking in shorts and tank top but thought it best to just ask for food. Stick to the essentials. That's what her husband, Greg, had always drummed into her. "I was wondering if I could buy any leftovers from yesterday. I know it's early and you're busy, but I'd be your friend for life if you could help me out here."

"Who is it, Dad?" A young woman's voice, sweeter than vanilla custard, called from the back of the room.

"One of them vet ladies who came to work at the track," he called back, his eyes never leaving Maggie's face. "You know, the ones who found Craig dead on the crapper."

From the back of the room, a petite woman in her late twenties, also dressed in a white coat but minus the hat, came forward, smiling. "Hi, I'm Candy. Don't take any notice of my father. He has no idea of tact. I'm trying to teach him to act like a civilized human being but so far, I haven't succeeded." She tipped her head on one side. "Are you lost?"

"No. It's just-um-well, you see, I have an early morning meeting with um-a *friend* who isn't in a good mood and I was wondering if you had any pastries I could buy as a peace offering."

"Sounds intriguing." Candy's smile widened. "How about I make you up a six pack of donuts and add one of my special apple pies to sweeten the deal?"

Donuts and apple pie? Oh, be quiet my beating heart. Maggie returned the girl's grin, her nose zeroing in on the enticing smell of apple pie that wafted from the kitchen. "Thanks, Candy," she said, trying unsuccessfully to curb the growls of anticipation emanating from her empty stomach. "That sounds perfect."

Money quickly changed hands and Maggie continued on down the street, her treasure trove of goodies looking much more enticing—even after she'd sampled a piece of Candy's apple pie and two chocolate donuts that virtually jumped into her mouth.

By the time she arrived at the caravan park a shy sun had woken, stretched its rays outwards and was now peeping over the horizon. The sky, in anticipation of another baking hot day, basked in every shade of red, yellow and orange that graced the color-wheel of Nature.

Invigorated by her early morning walk, Maggie paused to drag in a lungful of fresh sweet smelling air—held it for the count of ten—and slowly let it out again.

A vocal family of magpies, unperturbed by her presence, dug their sharp pointed beaks into the soft dew on the lawn surrounding the park. Looking for bugs? Worms? Or whatever it was magpies the world over searched for in newly mown grass.

Life was good.

And then, without warning, a sharp stab of misery sliced its way through her chest forcing her to catch her breath. Yes, life *was* good but it could be snuffed out in a millisecond. Like the lowlife who'd stolen Greg's life, leaving her with an empty space in her bed and in her heart. And no matter what the sleazy Craig Benham had been guilty of in *his* life, no-one had the right to take it away from him.

No one.

She pushed the park gate open and the sudden negative thoughts from her mind. Time to wake Barry and twist his arm with the promise of food and find out if he knew what was going on in this hot haven of ambiguity called Kangaroo Downs.

Barry's caravan was situated at the back of the site in an isolated corner surrounded by thick bushes. As Maggie drew closer she could hear raised voices coming from inside. Barry, arguing defensively, and she didn't recognize the other voice. Not wanting to be seen, Maggie ducked in behind the bushes to listen. Whoever was arguing with Barry was either throwing things around inside the van or thumping his fist against the wall to highlight his displeasure.

Was it Mr. Chang, Barry's landlord, demanding rent money? But surely he wouldn't have reason to get *this* angry. All he had to do was tell Barry to move out and if he refused, ask the police to intervene.

Maggie frowned as another object crashed against the wall inside the van. Maybe she should ring the police. But would they worry about Barry? Maybe they'd think he deserved what he was getting. It was evidently someone Barry had upset. The owner of a fence he'd graffitied? A guy whose car he'd stolen for a joy ride? An angry shopkeeper?

And where was Barry's racing dog? Surely Rocky wasn't inside the van while all this was going on. The dog could be lying inside, hurt. Maggie crept from her hiding place and snuck around to the front of the van, using the bushes to keep hidden.

She let out a sigh of relief and smiled. There was Rocky tied to a stake out the front under a tree with a bowl of water and a blanket.

"Hi Rocky," she whispered as she approached the dog.

Rocky's tail gave an apprehensive wag.

"Seems like your owner is in a spot of trouble."

Maggie swore the dog rolled its eyes at her.

"I *was* going to pay him a visit. Share donuts and apple pie with him. But considering the activity inside that van at the moment I think I might just wait here for a bit and see what happens."

Rocky agreed. He snuggled his head into Maggie's hand for a pat and invited her to sit on his blanket, maybe share a donut, or three.

"At least Barry had the good sense to put you outside so you can't get hurt," she told the smooching greyhound and then shook her head in bemusement. What the hell was she doing talking to a dog?

"Idiot!" A thunderous yell, so loud it sent a flock of ibises scattering, blared through the window of the van and made Maggie flinch. "I told you to keep the fuck away from them. And what do you do? You bring them back here and let them find the red paint." Maggie's mouth gaped. He was talking about Emily and her. "And now the bitches are asking questions around town."

"I didn't know you'd put it under my van." Barry's voice had developed a whine. "And I didn't *let* them find the paint. *She* found it. The nosy one. It was *her* fault."

Absently patting Rocky's head, Maggie frowned. *The nosy one?* That hurt, especially as she'd been feeling sorry for the little toe-rag. She had to move closer. Get a look inside the van. Find out who the blaspheming charmer was with his jock strap in a twisted knot.

Maybe she should just knock on the door and offer them both donuts.

A balled-up fist hit the caravan wall followed by a string of oaths that would have done a resident of cell block 3 proud.

Or maybe not…

Crouched low, heart clogging her throat at the thought of being caught by the maniac inside, Maggie ran, bent double, across the grass. Damn. The van was on blocks and even on tip-toe the window was too high to reach. After attempting a couple of unsuccessful high jumps, she glanced around for something solid to stand on. And shook her head. Unless she borrowed a sledge hammer and busted the cement around the wooden park bench then dragged that over—there was nothing suitable to stand on.

She was just contemplating either dialing 000 or climbing a tree for a better view when the caravan door burst open. Tortured hinges screamed in protest and then the whole door took off, air-borne, and landed three feet away.

Holy Toledo! Time for her to do a disappearing act. Fast.

While John Taylor, alias Hairy Guy, alias Ape, was busy booting Barry's pot plants and inventing colorful new swear words, Maggie threw herself down on the ground and quickly rolled under the van out of sight. From there she could only see Ape's legs and feet so she wriggled forward to get a better view.

After kicking the last of Barry's pot plants over, Ape shook his fist in the air. "Last warning, Pea-brain," he roared. "If I hear you've been gabbing your mouth off to them bitches again, you'll be eating your food through a straw. Got it?"

Maggie winced at the thought of Barry with broken teeth then let out a shaky sigh. This lumbering, bad-tempered guy with a body hair problem was evidently responsible for sabotaging the track's opening.

But had he also killed Craig Benham, the track's Chief Steward?

And if so, why?

Flat on her stomach eating dirt, Maggie watched John Taylor, the man they called Ape, storm off toward the Truck-stop Diner's delivery truck which he'd parked behind a hedge on the opposite side of the park. Before she could escape however, Barry, white faced, almost in tears, flew from the van. In his hand he grasped what looked like a broken toaster which he hauled off and threw at the departing bully. Then, bouncing up and down amid the wreck of his smashed front door and trashed flowers he let forth with a litany of curly obscenities.

At least the kid looked okay. No evidence of broken bones or major blood spills. Maggie sighed into the dirt.

No reason to call an ambulance…yet.

Playing doggo, Maggie waited until the truck pulled away and Barry, still making up new curse words, rescued the now trembling Rocky and decided to take the dog for a walk.

Thank you, God.

Joints badly in need of oiling, Maggie rolled out from under the van, clambered to her feet, rescued the squashed bakery bag and decided her best course of action was to return to the B&B.

After that little episode she knew it would take a lot more than squashed donuts and apple pie to encourage Barry to talk.

23

Is it Ape?

Emily speared another bite of crispy, heavenly smelling bacon with her fork and waved it at Lola who'd brought breakfast forward an hour after both Emily and Maggie had returned looking the worse for wear. "So, as much as my gut says *no way*—because David is one hell of a nice guy *and* he helped save the life of your cat," Emily told Lola between bites. "You have to admit he has a good motive for shooting Craig Benham. In *his* mind Craig was instrumental in killing his wife."

"Can't see it, myself," said Lola hovering over their table with a steaming hot pot of coffee while keeping one eye on her other guests. "The tragedy with David's wife happened over a year ago. I remember how devastated he was at the time and okay he *did* threaten to kill Craig—but why would he wait until now?"

Maggie looked up, a dob of egg on her chin. "Sounds to me like the classic cuckolded husband waiting for the right opportunity," she said as she scooped another heaped forkful of egg from her plate and transferred it into her mouth with a blissful sigh.

Emily lifted one eyebrow at her friend and grinned. It was always a pleasure to watch Maggie eat. This everyday task was performed with such gusto, such delight, such utter abandon it was almost sensual. Whether she ate a meal in front of the television dressed in baggy sweats or at a five-hundred-dollar Charity function wearing the latest fashion creation, Maggie Post always enjoyed her food.

"Maybe," said Lola leaning over to top up Emily's coffee cup. "But I don't think so. When the Ashford's first arrived in Kangaroo Downs, David worked his butt off all hours of the day and night to establish his veterinary practice while Mrs. High-and-Mighty Stephanie fluttered around town like a fairy tale Princess. If she'd had any backbone she'd have been down and dirty helping her husband, instead of fluttering right into Craig Benham's bed. Of course once Craig finished screwing both her and her money, he tossed her out on her skinny butt. She couldn't take it and drove over a cliff to show Craig how much she loved him." Lola shook her head in disgust. "Even if I live to be a hundred and six and grow a beard, I'll *never* understand that soppy thinking. No male is worth taking your own life."

With a snort of conviction, Emily agreed. Every time she thought of Peter and his indiscretions it still managed to hurt like the twisting of a knife, but no way would she ever take her own life because of his rejection. "David told me his wife was mentally unstable at the time of her death."

"Which might explain Steph's actions," replied Lola. "But it still doesn't explain why David would wait this long for retribution."

Emily finished her bacon and started in on the crisp-on-the-outside-butter-soft-on-the-inside hash browns.

"Perfect, aren't' they?" said Maggie who must have noticed Emily's glazed expression. "Grease. Glorious grease. Best way to kick off a morning."

"Especially after performing a two hour complicated veterinary operation," agreed Emily. "Anyway, my money's on this Ape guy as being the murderer. After what Maggie heard and saw this morning, everything points to the big guy with the excess hair problem. He's definitely the saboteur—so why not the murderer too?" Emily waved her fork again. "Picture this. We know the deceased was the manager of the Kangaroo Down's racing club, so it's more than likely he'd be at the track inspecting the equipment, checking for problems that might interfere with a successful opening day. Especially considering how many things had already gone wrong leading up to the opening. Anyway, he comes across this Ape guy gumming up the works on the starting barriers—or whatever—threatens to report him to the police, so our boy Ape shoots Craig, drags him into the delivery van and deposits the body in Joe and Jean's restrooms. That way, maybe the police will think it was a random act of murder and nothing to do with the race track. Or him."

Maggie frowned. "But would Ape be carrying a gun while dismantling the starting barriers?"

Emily screwed up her nose, thought about this for a couple of seconds, and then shrugged before continuing. "Anyway…he could even have been trying to frame Joe by leaving the body at the diner. Doesn't seem much love lost between those two. When Ape and Bazza came into the diner while we were waiting for the police to arrive, I thought Joe was going to throw a punch at the guy."

"You're right there," said Lola, indicating with one finger for the guests at the other table to hang on one minute. "Joe can't stand Ape but Jean's the one who employs him part time—mostly for deliveries and any heavy work. And I wouldn't be surprised if she also employs him to warm her bed on the odd occasion that Joe's out doing an all-nighter, delivering orders to Port Augusta or Whyalla."

Maggie almost choked on her bacon. "Jean and Ape? You're kidding."

"No. The woman can't help herself—she's a sexomaniac."

Emily buried her smile in her coffee cup. "You mean she suffers from hyper sexuality?"

"That too. *And* she's a nympho," huffed Lola. "I heard on the grapevine Craig's wife was threatening to file for divorce so maybe Craig wanted to break it off with Jean. Maybe that's why Jean had been making goo-goo eyes at young Ape."

"Craig's *wife*?" Emily did a double-take. No one had bothered to mention the dead man had a *wife*.

"This just gets juicier and juicier," said Maggie through a mouthful of hash browns. She raised an eyebrow at Emily. "Maybe we should go ask *Mrs.* Craig a few questions."

"Lucy Benham lives on a property twenty miles out of town," said Lola over her shoulder as she hurried off to attend to her other guests. "But you'd better wear your bullet proof vests because Mad Lucy has been known to shoot first and ask questions later. Not a great lover of strangers, our Lucy."

"Damn," said Emily, arranging her knife and fork on top of her empty plate and frowning across at Maggie. "Bullet proof vests are the only things we forgot to pack."

24

Trouble at the Workshop

Aaah… now this was more like it!

Emily smiled as four hours later she and Maggie delivered lectures under a covered betting-ring at the soon-to-be-opened Kangaroo Downs race-track. Her smile widened as she surveyed the enthusiastic owners, trainers and various others who'd initially appeared just for the food and drink but found themselves caught up in the excitement. And why wouldn't they be? Everyone here today, if they listened, could take home new ideas and procedures on the best way to breed, care for, and train a thoroughbred race horse.

The morning workshop was humming along like clockwork. Emily beamed across at Maggie who grinned back at her. Perhaps this star-crossed assignment might turn out a success after all. Already Tony Matthews, leading Northern trainer and owner of Kangaroo Lodge, had answered dozens of questions from the audience about training methods, while Emily had demonstrated the best method of inserting an IV injection, lectured on knee surgery together with after-care treatment and during Maggie's lecture on line-breeding for speed and strength, the listeners were full of questions.

The late-morning sun, its harsh rays picking out dust motes and turning them into tiny cobwebby rainbows, slanted through both ends of the betting-ring and came to rest on an elegant grey thoroughbred mare called Jell-O, the model for Emily's current demonstration on the correct method of applying support bandages. Emily breathed in deeply. The only thing she loved more than the smell of hay and earth and fresh air, was the smell of horse.

Teena, the teenaged girl they'd seen reading a book while swimming a horse in the Kangaroo Lodge Stud's circular horse pool the day before, held the horse's halter in light but firm hands. The owner of the Lodge, Tony Matthews, had loaned his daughter, Teena, and the elegant grey mare for the day's workshop.

While Emily bent to sort the bandages needed for her talk, Teena slipped the mare a peppermint and whispered encouragement in the horse's ear. "Not much longer, Jell-O."

"Is she always so well-behaved?" Emily asked straightening up with a set of iridescent pink bandages tucked under one arm. The pink would look stunning against the horse's grey legs.

"Jell-O's one special horse," Teena said, and rubbed a hand down the horse's long nose. "Even when she was still racing the jockeys used to fight over her because she was so easy to ride. Her two foals, one a two-year old and the other a yearling, are just as even-tempered as their mum."

"I must say, it's been a pleasure working with her." Emily patted the mare's sleek neck. "Some of the horses I've treated at the Equine Clinic in Adelaide would have picked me up in their teeth and shaken me by now. Your mare has let me bend her knees in all directions, demonstrate the best techniques for inserting an intravenous injection, stood quietly while I've answered questions and just now when she saw me sorting bandages she gave me that resigned look as if to say, what is this mad woman going to do to me next?"

Teena laughed. "Looked like she was taking a nap through your talk about intravenous injections but she soon woke up when you demonstrated on her."

"Well, at least applying a support bandage won't hurt," Emily told Jell-O, pulling on one of the horse's ears before turning to her audience.

This was Emily's last lecture for the day to be followed by Maggie presentation on the benefits and techniques of massage.

Surely nothing could go wrong now.

"The reason we use exercise bandages while working a race-horse is to provide support for the horse's lower leg and to protect them from knocks," she told her audience. "So, today I'm going to show you the correct way to wrap an exercise bandage."

Emily held up a Gamgee pad. "In my opinion, the best cushioning to use under a support bandage is a Fybagee or Gamgee, but you can use neoprene leg-wraps, a roll of cotton-wool, or even quilting," she said. "One thing, before I start this demonstration, I want to point out that all bandages should be removed straight after the horse has been worked and must never be left on or unchecked for long periods."

"Why?"

Emily smiled at the jockey-sized guy who'd asked the question. He was standing in front of the track secretary, Charles Norton-Phillips, who had positioned himself in a prominent position near the workshop speakers. It was then she noticed Ape, as he pushed past the jockey-sized questioner to whisper something in Charles's ear. Something that made Charles's eyes bug and his face turn an unhealthy shade of red.

Hmm... evidently Ape hadn't complimented Charles on his choice of bow tie.

One eye on the two combatants, Emily answered the man's question. "If left on too long the legs could swell under the bandages, restrict blood flow or potentially damage tendons and then you'd have more problems."

Emily watched as Charles shoved Ape in the chest, snarled, and then stood up, his chair toppling over backwards in his hurry to get away. As though enjoying the other man's discomfort, Ape laughed. He stood there for a moment, mouth twisted in a smarmy grin, hair an out-of-control bush well past its pruning date. And then he disappeared in the crowd.

As the girl who fell down the rabbit-hole famously said: 'Curiouser and curiouser...'

"The bandage should be fitted just below the knee or hock to just above the fetlock joint," Emily continued struggling to keep her mind on the lecture. She bent down to run a hand over Jell-O's left front leg, laying the hair flat. Almost like she knew how important she was, Jell-O stood taller, head high, expression regal as Emily continued her demonstration. "Place the cushioning against the leg, and, starting on the inside or outside, wrap the chosen padding around the leg working from front to back, finishing on the outside. Then, start bandaging from the top of the padding with the bandage facing front to back leaving a spare tab of approximately three inches above the padding."

Emily glanced across to where Charles and Ape had disappeared but there was no sign of either of them. Maggie, who'd been sitting next to Charles, raised her eyebrows at Emily and nodded as if to say… *I've got something to tell you when this is over.* Shaking her head, Emily continued bandaging Jell-O's front leg, instructing the class on how to fold down the tab and do the second turn over the top to secure the end.

"It's important to keep the pressure even all the way down and ensure there are no wrinkles in either the bandage or the padding."

After returning up the leg she showed how to keep the ties flat and wrap them around the leg then fold the top half of the first turn to cover the knot. "Now, we'll secure the bandage with two strips of tape and that's it. No magic involved—just common sense and practice."

"What about using boots instead of bandages?" asked a bespectacled male sitting on a bookmaker's stand near the back. "Can horse-boots do the same thing?"

While a few were old hands at training race-horses, many were first time owners, trainers or stable-hands, all eager to participate in the sport now their town had its own race track. These were the people Emily found the most enthusiastic. "Of course. There are many low-priced *and* exorbitantly priced horse-boots on the market today. And yes, they will do the job and are less time consuming. Especially if you have several horses in work," she said, "but boots don't mold to the horse's legs like a support bandage." Emily looked around at the interested faces and smiled. "Now if there are no more questions, I'll step aside and let my friend, Maggie Post instruct you on the intricacies of massage."

Maggie stood up ready to take Emily's place.

"Thank you, Jell-O." Emily gently tugged on the horse's ear and accepted a soft, wet, velvety nose to her cheek in return. "You too, Teena. You've been as patient as your beautiful horse."

"Hey, did you see Mr. Norton-Philipps shove Ape?" Teena grinned and shook her head. "Thought our illustrious secretary was going to pop his bow-tie."

"Any idea why they'd be arguing?"

Teena shrugged. "Nope, but Ape's a bit of a loser. Used to work for us a couple of days a week but Dad gave him the boot when he found him helping himself to the petty cash."

"What about the other one?"

"Chunky Charles?" Teena's infectious laugh made Emily grin. "My dad can't stand him either. Reckons he's a two-bit phony."

Emily laughed. "Two-bit phony?"

"Yeah," Teena smiled at Maggie as she ambled over and then turned back to Emily. "Dad says Mr. Norton-Phillips owes people money yet he acts like he's rich and famous."

"Your dad sounds a very perceptive guy." Emily turned away from Teena and deliberately bumped against Maggie as they changed places. "Hear anything?" she whispered.

"Tell you later," muttered Maggie and slung one around the grey mare's neck. "Hi, Jell-O. Ready for a rub down? You'll enjoy it, I promise. Probably be snoring half way through."

The horse appeared happy with the arrangement, so Maggie turned to speak to her audience. "In my opinion, the first thing you should do after track-work or a race is cool your horse down and then give him a gentle massage. Why? Because massage as a therapy has been around for centuries, it's useful for the prevention and cure of injuries, it improves circulation and—best of all—it promotes well-being and relaxation." She rolled her eyes, gave an exaggerated sigh and then flashed her disarming grin at the audience. "Hey, maybe we should employ someone to give trainers and jockeys a massage after the race too."

The audience tittered and while Maggie began using the heels of both hands and her fingers to knead the mare's neck, Emily joined in the laughter. She reached across, opened their vet bag and peered inside searching for the bottle of massage oil they'd made up especially for the workshop today. What the heck? It was gone.

Hand outstretched for the oil, Maggie half turned to her audience. "Emily and I have our own special recipe for massage oil and if you'd like a printed copy just come and see one of us at the end of the session." She glanced across at Emily. "Can you pass the bottle please, Em?"

Emily shook her head, bewildered. She remembered dropping the bottle of oil into her bag before they'd left for the workshop. So where was it now?

A loud snigger caught her attention. She frowned and looked up in time to see Ape grinning at her from a few meters away. The moment he'd caught her attention, he walked off again, his back shaking with suppressed laughter.

Oh no! What was the guy with the excessive hair problem up to now? Since arriving in Kangaroo Downs he'd turned into their worst nightmare. She wouldn't trust John Taylor as far as she could push him up a hill in a bottomless wheelbarrow.

"Ah, there it is." Maggie gave a small self-deprecating laugh as she spotted the missing bottle standing on the table behind the computer. "Think I need to visit an optician." She snagged the dark bottle and gave it a shake before screwing off the lid. "Now, I'll just tip a little of this mixture onto my hands to make it easier to massage and warm the horse's muscles."

Emily frowned. Something wasn't right. *She* hadn't taken the bottle out of her bag. And evidently Maggie hadn't or she wouldn't have been surprised to find it on the table. So who did?

And then the snigger made sense. The reason Ape had disappeared, laughing like a loon, fell into place.

Ape, the saboteur, had been at work again. But what did he add to their bottle of massage oil? Draino? Poison? Itchy powder?

Oh my God. Maggie, unaware of the danger was chatting away to her audience as she tilted the bottle, ready to spread the oil over her hands. With a gasp, Emily threw herself across the space and snatched the bottle from Maggie's hands. "Um, sorry, Mags," she choked, looking around for the lid. "I think I might have added a tad too much um…wintergreen. How about using Penetrene as a liniment today?"

For a moment Maggie's eyes glazed in confusion and then understanding registered. She narrowed her eyes and frowned. "Penetrene's fine. In fact, any oil will do, even baby oil," she went on, always the showman. "It's only a lubricant to help the hands slide over the horse's muscles more easily."

With that, she smiled at the audience, accepted the Penetrene from Emily and continued with her demonstration.

Emily lifted the suspect bottle to her nose and sniffed. Good grief! Ape had added cayenne pepper to the mixture while no-one was looking. A bubble of anger churned and stewed and grew into a full-sized tempest in the pit of her stomach. Anyone who could hurt a beautiful trusting animal like Jell-O *and* laugh about it could also be responsible for putting a gun to Craig Benham's head and pulling the trigger. Swallowing the bile that threatened to choke her, Emily steadied her shaking hands.

The moment this workshop was over she would hunt down the unfeeling, insensitive, low-life creep. No matter where he was—no matter what he was doing. And when she did, she'd throw the contents of the sabotaged bottle at him, making sure the fiery liquid landed precisely where it would do the most damage.

25

Hunting Ape

Maggie ran a hand through her sweaty hair as the heat of the early afternoon sun burned through the cotton of her blouse and thin cotton slacks. She'd left the shade of the betting-ring to bid farewell to the last of the workshop attendees and the temperature hovered around 39-40 degrees. Even the birds in the nearby trees were silent. She grimaced. If she had as much sense as the birds she wouldn't be standing out in the sun, she'd be snoozing, head under wing, perched on the bough of a shady tree—or maybe curled up with a cold drink on an inflated mattress beneath that shady tree.

Wriggling in an attempt to lever the sweaty material away from her damp skin, she couldn't stop the big smile from lifting the corners of her mouth. Hey, the sun was a kicker, but not even the oppressive heat could tamp down the adrenaline sizzling through her bloodstream. This workshop had been a resounding success. And she'd proven to herself and her friend, Emily, that she was ready to move on with her life and be a useful partner of *Vets2U*.

Still on a high, Maggie's smile broadened as she glanced across at Emily—and did a double-take. Emily was edging away from the last of the workshop attendees, a talkative husband and wife team. Blinking in confusion, Maggie watched her friend shift impatiently from one foot to the other before finally taking off. Geez, her friend was almost running. What on earth was wrong with her? This was *so* not like Emily.

Emily Harrison was the professional side of their newly formed partnership and normally she'd go out of her way to answer clients' questions.

The garrulous couple threw another question in Emily's direction but instead of slowing down she merely tossed the answer over her left shoulder, beckoned Maggie to follow her, and kept going.

Maggie scowled at Emily's retreating back and shook her head. Breaking speed records on a 40-degree day was *so* not her idea of fun but Emily had her bee in a bonnet about something so she had no choice but to follow her. After a couple of minutes of lumbering Maggie put on an extra spurt and grabbed Emily by the arm. "Hey, where's the fire?" Her breath sounded louder than a steam train.

"We're hunting Ape," said Emily as she shook herself free from Maggie's grip. "Now, tell me, what happened between Ape and Charles during the workshop? Did you hear anything?"

"Not much. Ape bumped into me and sent my chair flying and I was rather preoccupied with saving myself."

"You must have heard something?"

"All I heard was Ape demanding ten thousand dollars and I didn't catch the rest. I was too busy struggling to keep my chair upright." Maggie lifted her elbow where a bruise was starting to form. "This is the result of Ape crashing into my chair so hard that my elbow connected with the corner of the table."

"Hmm…ten thousand dollars?" echoed Emily, evidently not interested in Maggie's bruise. She frowned, a thoughtful expression on her face. "Maybe Ape's a blackmailer as well as a saboteur. Maybe he's also guilty of murdering Craig Benham," she continued, now on a roll. "Craig caught him in the act of smashing the infrastructure at the track, or wrecking the starting barriers, or tampering with the electricity, threatened to go to the police, so Ape shot him."

Cold prickles ran up Maggie's spine. Rubbing her hands up and down her arms, she shivered. "Tell you what…there's a creepy undercurrent in this wacky town. Could film the next crime series here."

"You're spot on there," Emily said and increased her speed. "Now, let's find Ape. He's probably doing whatever last-minute damage he can to stop the race-meeting from going ahead tomorrow."

"But you just said he's a blackmailer, a saboteur and a murderer. So why would we want to find Ape?"

"So I can hurt him."

"What?"

"Slime-ball added cayenne pepper to our massage oil. That maggot fully intended to burn Jell-O's skin just so he could disrupt the workshop."

"Cayenne pepper?" Maggie felt her mouth open and shut. Her heart skipped a beat. She remembered during her lecture, just before Emily grabbed the bottle away from her, she'd been upending the bottle ready to tip the massage oil onto her hands. "Holy hen's teeth! That was close. Are you sure it was Ape?"

"It was definitely Ape. You didn't see the smirk on his face, Mags. I did." Emily growled deep in her throat and took off in the direction of the horse-stalls. "I want to find him and tip the contents of this bottle somewhere where the sun never shines."

"Be careful, Em," said Maggie scurrying to keep up. Her friend was a feisty cock-sparrow but Maggie had seen and heard Ape in action. He was a nasty piece of work *and* he played dirty. "I think we should go to the police with what we already know and leave it up to them to sort out this whole mystery. Senior Constable Mark Kelly seems very efficient."

"And what do we tell him? You happened to be nearby and saw John Taylor throwing things around in Barry Sullivan's caravan and threatening him? Constable Kelly would laugh. Probably an everyday occurrence." Emily snorted through her nose. "And what evidence do we have that he *did* interfere with the bottle of massage oil or that he's responsible for sabotaging the race track. Or that he's a murderer. A smirk, a fight and an overheard remark which he'd deny? It would be his word against ours. And we're outsiders."

Maggie sighed. When did life get so complicated?

As they passed the race-caller's tower and moved toward the sound of hammering which appeared to be coming from behind the horse stalls, Emily grabbed Maggie's arm and pulled her to a stop. "Mags, I need more on this guy before fronting up to the police, okay? I need enough evidence for them to throw the book at him. Are you with me?"

"I guess so." Maggie gave a half-hearted one-shoulder shrug. After witnessing Ape in action at the caravan park, she wasn't too keen on confronting him without back-up. Or at the very least, a big heavy stick. She glanced around the track and shivered. Where were all the people from the workshop when you needed them? Drinking at the bar or on their way home to care for their horses in the heat, she supposed. The only humans in sight were a family of three walking out the gate and a man driving a tractor on the far side of the track.

What if whoever was wielding that hammer behind the horse stalls was the murderer himself? Maggie put a finger to her mouth to keep Emily quiet and slowed down their approach. A hammer could be a mighty fine weapon in the hands of killer.

"Hold it, Em," she whispered in her friend's ear. "Let's check out who's doing the hammering before we confront them. If it's Ape, I'm not accusing him of anything without first weighing my handbag down with rocks. Greg's told me about guys like him. When they're cornered they don't care who they hurt."

Emily, chin jutting forward, kept walking.

Frustrated, Maggie fastened on to the back of Emily's shirt and towed her closer to the stable wall. "Trust me, Em. This is *not* the correct way to approach a violent suspect. Let's just check the perp out first without him seeing us. Find out if he's armed or if he has an accomplice with him," she warned. "And I still say we should ring the police."

"Okay, okay, we'll do it your way…but no police. Not yet. We need evidence of this guy committing a crime first." Emily bent down and picked up a jagged rock from the path, weighed it in her hand and then leaned against the stable wall. "Did you bring your phone?"

"Yes, and if he's up to no good I'll take a video of him committing the crime and *then* we'll ring the police. We do not approach him ourselves." Maggie spoke slowly, emphasizing each word. "Right?"

Emily screwed her nose in displeasure and the frustrated eye-roll reminded Maggie so much of her teenage daughter, Judy, she had to stifle a giggle.

The hammering came from behind the horse stalls, so Maggie edged along the galvanized iron wall, phone at the ready, until she reached the corner. With bated breath she poked first her nose around the corner, and then her phone and lastly the rest of her head.

"I can't see what's happening," complained Emily, crowding her from behind. "What's he doing? Have you taken a photo yet?"

"Em, don't push!" Maggie growled but she may as well have spoken to the sky. Another impatient shove from Emily and she felt herself pitch forward. "Nooo!" Arms and legs flailing uselessly in an attempt to retain her balance, Maggie knew staying upright was a battle she had no chance of winning. With a thud that robbed her of her breath, she hit the dirt, belly first. Her phone flew in a high arc before joining her on the ground with an ominous clunk. And she closed her eyes in surrender.

All she could hope was that John Taylor, alias Ape, had left his gun at home tucked away in his biscuit barrel, and not in the back pocket of his jeans.

26

In Barrier Two

What a monumental screw-up!

Maggie held her breath and squeezed her eyes tightly shut. She could sense someone standing over her and by the rank smell of week-old sweat, figured it wasn't her friend, Emily.

A foot shuffled in the dirt beside her. Oh, God, it was Ape and he was going to kick her in the head with his iron-toed work boots. Why hadn't Emily listened when she told her they should leave this to the police? She cringed, gritted her teeth, tensed ready for the oncoming pain and prayed he didn't aim at her nose. A broken nose and blood wouldn't look good when the police discovered her corpse buried in a shallow grave beside the winning post.

The foot shuffled again…

Then silence.

Okay, lying doggo with her eyes shut wasn't achieving squat. So…time to initiate plan B. Even if Ape didn't have a gun, he could still sink his boots in and while she was screaming 'enough' he could pick up the sledge-hammer and batter her to death. She fisted her hands and stiffened her spine. She'd rather see the murder-weapon coming and defend herself than die cowering on the ground with her eyes closed.

And what about Emily?

Her best friend might be feistier than a bag full of meerkats, but her 7-stone-two had no hope against a 200-pound gorilla like John Taylor.

Plus, Maggie couldn't protect Emily while she was sprawled in the dirt. Or could she? She recalled one of the many martial-art defenses Greg had taught her over the years to keep her safe. If she was ever knocked over by a potential mugger or a rapist he'd shown her how to bring the attacker down from a prone position—how to take him by surprise—how to wrap both arms around his knees and bring him to the ground, like felling a tree. Maybe that would work on Ape.

She had to try.

But first she needed to know how close her attacker was so she could plan her moves. Muscles tense, she unglued her eyes a smidgen, just enough to identify the blur of a male shape standing beside her. Hmm…Ape looked skinnier than the last time she'd seen him. She cracked her eyes open another couple of notches until she was looking up into two anxious dark eyes and a youthful face adorned with more metal than an iron kettle.

"Oh, God, it's *you!*" Maggie pushed herself into a sitting position and sent her glare upwards. "What are *you* doing here, Barry, and where's your scumbag mate?" Her eyes fell on his tightly fisted left hand. "And what's with the hammer?" She could see sheets of iron on the ground, evidently ripped off the back of the horse stalls. Disappointment as thick and smothering as a blanket caught hold of her. This boy who they'd tried to help wasn't worth their angst after all. "I'll never fathom your reasoning Barry," she said to him. "Even with a job offer at this track, you're still causing damage in an effort to close it down. And for what? A shitload of dirty money? An adrenalin rush?" Her stomach pitched in revulsion and she shook her head. "I give up, Barry. You're not worth the angst."

Emily stretched out a hand and helped Maggie to her feet. "Sorry, Mags. You okay? I just couldn't see what was happening back there and when I tried to move you out the way, you sort of lost your balance."

"Move me out the way?" Maggie's mouth gaped. "Emily, you barged straight into me and sent me flying."

Emily bent to pick up Maggie's phone, grimaced and then handed it over with a shrug. "Sorry, again. Looks like either the battery's flat or it's um…broken."

Maggie shook her phone, clicked it a couple of times and when nothing happened rammed it into her pocket with a sigh.

"Don't worry," Emily said and smiled. "I can always take an incriminating photo or video on *my* phone."

Maggie's sigh lengthened.

"What's going on?" Barry seemed to come out of his stunned amazement and as he spoke he waved the hammer in the air. "You two have been spying on me, haven't you?"

"Hey, drop that weapon, young man," snapped Emily, "before you do something you'll regret. Something that'll put you behind bars until you're ready to collect the old-aged pension."

Barry looked down at the hammer in his hand as though he'd forgotten it was there. He shrugged one shoulder. "Are you outta ya tree, lady? I'm not threatening you. I've been hammering nails into this sheet of iron." When Emily's glare refused to waver, he dropped the hammer on the ground and put both hands out, palms first, for her to inspect. "Hey, all I'm doing is fixing the back of the horse stall."

"Oh yeah," said Maggie. "And how did it get *un*fixed?"

Barry squirmed and scratched at the metal rings piercing his nose. "Well…you see, Ape told me to meet him at the horse stalls and when he got here he was all hyped up and laughing and going on about money and getting' outta this lousy town. Then he just sorta went mental and started ripping off the back of the horse stalls with a crowbar. Tried to, like, get me to help him, but I wouldn't. I went to stop him and he clobbered me. Then he got this phone call and started swearing. Said he had a job to do at the starting barriers and left. And before you ask me, no, I don't know what he planned to do. He didn't tell me. Anyway, when he took off I decided to nail the sheets of iron back up again."

Maggie cocked her head on one side, waited until the boy looked her in the eye and frowned at him. "How can we believe you, Barry, when all this time you've been helping Ape to sabotage the track?"

Barry chewed on his bottom lip, bravado warring with tears until finally he shrugged his thin shoulders. "Ape threatened to kill my dog, Rocky, if I didn't do as he said."

Oh God. Maggie's virtuous anger dissipated like a pricked balloon. This kid didn't need censure—he needed friends. People who cared for him.

"So why have you changed your mind now?" asked Emily.

Barry's face lit up. "You know, Dion, from the fodder store?"

"Aaah…yes…I've met the memorable Dion." Emily blew out a breath and fanned her face.

Maggie stifled a laugh at the bewildered look on Barry's face before he blinked at Emily and then went on. "Well, you see, Dion trains greyhounds too and he said if I help him with his dogs I can live in a shed at the back of the store until I can get a full-time job and save the money to rent a place of my own." His grin broadened. "Rocky's there now. He's safe, so that's why I can stand up to Ape."

"Good for you." Maggie reached out and squeezed Barry's shoulder. He was just a young boy who'd come close to turning bad because of a rotten apple's influence. "Come here," she said and threw one arm around his shoulders. "I'm glad you have Dion on your side now but believe me when I say John Taylor is not going to hurt you or your dog ever again. With you as witness and the evidence we'll find when we check out whatever that creep is up to over at the starting barriers, the police will put him away where he can't hurt you anymore. Okay?"

Barry's thin body, stiffer than a fence post under her arm, gradually relaxed. "You think so?"

"I *know* so."

"That's if there's anything left of the hairy scumbag after I accidently spill this bottle of hot massage oil over him," put in Emily. "Now, come on you two, time's ticking. Let's go catch the saboteur in the act, take a video, and then ring the police."

When they reached the starting barriers which were on the opposite side of the track, there was no sign of Ape. In fact, this part of the track was empty. Possibly because it was quite a distance from the two most favored sites at any race track—the bar and the betting-ring. Even the solitary tractor driver they'd seen earlier had disappeared. Must have finished his or her job and gone home to a late lunch and a cold beer.

But where was Ape? Was he hiding nearby? Had he finished tampering with the barrier stalls in an effort to stop the races from going ahead tomorrow and then gone on to cause chaos elsewhere?

"Blimey, these look like they're straight from Hicksville," said Maggie standing behind the stalls and shaking her head in disbelief. The barrier stalls at Kangaroo Downs track were like no others she'd ever seen. Homemade box-like creations over six feet high and made from thick ply wood attached to metal frames.

"Ape and Craig smashed the new barrier stalls, so Arty Johnson, an old farmer mate of the Judge, made these up in a hurry so the track could open on time," said Barry coming up and standing beside them. "They've put in an order for a new set."

Maggie frowned. "What did you just say?"

"I said they've put in an order for a—"

"No, no. About Craig. You said *Craig* and Ape smashed the last set of barriers. But Craig was 'for' the opening of the track. He had race horses of his own and even helped the bill pass through. So why would he then go ahead and sabotage the track?"

"Dunno. Sorry. Just saw the two of them armed with sledge hammers one night smashing the barriers and carting them away in a big truck. They didn't see me and like I wasn't going to open my mouth, was I?"

"But why would Craig want to stop the track opening when he had so much invested in it?"

"And the big one," added Emily rolling her eyes. "If Craig was helping Ape, why would Ape kill him?"

"You're right. Doesn't add up."

"Unless Craig had a change of heart and told Ape he was going to turn himself into the police and report Ape too."

"Or Ape's not the murderer—just a saboteur and a blackmailer."

Walking closer to the back of the starting-barriers, Emily sniffed and wrinkled her nose at the sweet sickly smell that hung in the air. "Pheew! Ever noticed how in hot weather foul odors seem even more pungent?" She sniffed again and turned to Maggie. "Does that smell like cheap and nasty perfume to you? You know, the knock-off stuff with a well-known label affixed to the front."

"Yeah…maybe." Head reeling from Barry's new information and more interested in getting out of the heat than smelling cheap perfume, Maggie wiped stinging sweat from her eyes as she glanced up at the cloudless sky. "Geez, a shady tree would be nice right about now." The sun felt like it was burning a hole in her head and once again she'd left her hat behind.

Maggie let out a sigh and glanced across at the other two who looked almost as wilted as she felt. "Come on," she said and moved toward the first barrier stall, "let's see if we can discover what Ape's been up to. With the way his evil mind works it could be anything!"

She opened the first starting gate. Couldn't see any disturbance so moved onto the second one. Pity they hadn't been in time to catch their hirsute saboteur in the act and taken an incriminating photo of him. Still, with Barry's testimony and whatever Ape had been threatening Charles with they should have enough evidence to notify the police.

Emily swung open the gate to barrier three and eased herself inside for a closer scrutiny while Barry did the same to barrier four.

"Wish we knew what we were looking for," said Maggie as she reached out to open the gate on barrier two. Damn. It was stuck. She tugged harder. Nope, wouldn't move. And then a weird cold shiver skittered down her arms and the hairs stood up along the back of her neck. "Uh! Oh!" she growled and glanced across at the other two. "Looks like our friend, Mr. John Taylor may have been having his wicked way on this barrier stall."

"Here, let me help," Emily moved beside her, rubbed her hands together and then placed them, palms out, against the gate. "You're probably worn out from the heat, Mags. If I add my weight to yours, it'll open."

"Still say Ape's tampered with this one."

After pushing and heaving and finally breaking a nail, Emily stepped back and frowned at the gate. "Huh. You're right. Damn thing won't budge. Seems to be something wedged on the other side."

"Here, let me try." Barry stepped in front of them, flexed his muscles and grabbed the stubborn latch. Whether the latch had been loosened by their onslaught or Barry was stronger than he looked, when he gave stall number two an extra hard shove and wrenched the latch upwards, the gate swung open with a rush.

And out tumbled Ape's body.

"Oh! My! God!" Emily let out a strangled gasp. "Is he—?"

The depth of the bullet hole between Ape's staring eyes indicated that *yes*, he most certainly *was…*

27

Mad Lucy

"Constable Kelly needs a brain transplant," declared Emily with a snarl as she drove her Echo, all four wheels now intact, from the race track car park onto the main road. Her fingers strangled the steering wheel in a grip she'd like to transfer to Constable Kelly's scrawny neck. "How does Kelly figure Barry shot Ape? With his hammer? And anyway, Barry has an alibi. He was with us."

"Actually Barry doesn't have an alibi for the whole time," said Maggie staring out the car window. "Forensics will establish time of death was sometime between when Ape was last seen leaving the workshop and when we found him inside the starting barrier. He could have been murdered before we saw Barry." Maggie let out a frustrated sigh. She put one hand on Emily's arm and squeezed. "That's why Senior Constable Kelly allowed us to leave after we gave our statements but read Barry his rights and then hustled him off to the police station for more questioning."

"You think Barry—"

"No, of course not—but he *did* have motive and opportunity."

"So did everyone else at the track today," Emily snapped. She touched the brake with her foot, slowed at the corner to let half a dozen official looking cars, obviously forensics and crime scene experts, turn toward the Kangaroo Downs race-track, and scowled at the road ahead.

Emily wasn't sure why she was so upset about Barry being arrested for the murder of his hairy friend. Maybe it was the vulnerability, the sheer horror and grief in the boy's eyes when he'd opened the back of barrier two and they'd discovered Ape's body. Whatever it was, she knew Barry was innocent. She gripped the wheel tighter as a wave of frustration squeezed the muscles inside her chest. "So…who *did* kill Ape?"

"I don't know what to think any more," Maggie answered, scrubbing both hands across her eyes and shaking her head. "I've always believed I was a good judge of character, but since arriving in this town, my head hasn't stopped spinning. No-one here is who they appear to be on the surface. It's almost like we've been dropped in the middle of an Alfred Hitchcock movie—or a parallel universe." She shook her head. "But what I *do* know is I can't wait to get back to our B&B, stagger to the most comfortable chair in the establishment, collapse, kick off my shoes and let this nightmare pass me by while indulging in something so strongly alcoholic the glass threatens to shatter if I don't swig the contents down in three gulps."

As she drove, Emily tried to wrap her mind around the fact that the big ugly guy with the excessive hair—their chief suspect—was now himself a murder victim. And that young Barry was the main suspect. What about Charles Norton-Phillips? He had a good motive for killing Ape. And Joe hated his guts, as did half the citizens in this alien town. So how could she relax at the B&B knowing Barry was incarcerated in a cell for something he didn't do? She chewed on her bottom lip and frowned. Ever since Senior Constable Kelly had arrested Barry, handcuffed him, read him his rights and then driven off in the direction of the local police station, her nerves had been tighter than a wire stretched across the Grand Canyon.

Why? Because there was something drastically wrong with this trumped up scenario. Forcing her mind away from the what-ifs to what-to-do-next, she slowed the car down enough to screech around in a decidedly raggedy U-turn and head in the opposite direction.

Maggie, grabbing at the door handle let out a yell. "Emily Harrison, what the heck are you doing?"

"Okay, here's the plan," Emily said once they'd settled back onto the left side of the road. "Instead of driving to our B&B, where we'd merely sit and twiddle our thumbs for the rest of the day, we're going to pay a visit to Craig Benham's wife. Find out what she knows."

"We're *what*?"

Ha. That got Maggie's full attention. Her friend's eyes flew open and so did her mouth. "You and I are going to have a chat with the inimitable Mrs. Benham," Emily repeated, eyes firmly fixed on the road in front of her. "We can't just let young Barry sit in that jail wetting his pants with fear while we do nothing. Didn't you see the look he gave you when you told him not to worry about Rocky, we'd see he was fed and looked after tonight—just before that crabby old cop shoved him into the police car? It was like we were the only people in the world who might just care enough to believe in him."

"But *why* would you want to visit Mad Lucy Benham?"

"To question her of course. Find out where she was at the time of Ape's death." A chilling thought crept into Emily's mind. "*And* where she was at the time a bullet found its way into her husband's head."

Maggie laughed but it was so high pitched, for a moment Emily thought her friend was going to burst into tears. Or scream until her throat closed over. "Oh God," she finally croaked and her head slumped back on the headrest. "Do you realize you're turning into Miss Marple?" she said. "Younger and prettier of course—but still, Miss Marple?"

Emily grinned. "I'm glad you mentioned younger and prettier."

"It's no joke, Em. Why can't we leave the investigating to the police? That's their job."

"Because they won't even bother." Emily's voice gentled. She could tell her friend, like her, was close to the edge. "Come on, Mags, you saw the way the police treated Barry. As far as they're concerned they already have the guilty party in custody. Probably dump both murders onto him. Which means the real killer is still out there and could kill again. Bloody scary, if you ask me."

"It will be even scarier if this unknown killer doesn't like the idea of us interfering and decides to make us his next victims."

"So, in your opinion we should collect our belongings from *Emu's Bottom*, pack them in the car and then drive home with our tails between our legs. Leave poor Barry to the vultures. Is that really what you want to do?"

Maggie's face brightened momentarily and then her shoulders slumped in defeat. "Damn," she grumbled and Emily could almost see her hoisting a reluctant white flag in defeat. "Okay, you win. But if Mad Lucy decides to use us as target practice I'm going to grass you up to Saint Peter when we reach the Pearly Gates and inform him it was all your fault. Aren't you forgetting, Lola from the B&B said Craig's wife has a tendency to shoot first and ask questions later?"

"Okay…so we need a plan," said Emily ignoring the Saint Peter threat and Lola's dire warning. "You're the one with all the ideas so when we get to Benham's farm you'll know what to do." She grinned. "I'll just follow orders."

Maggie rolled her eyes and let out a strangled sigh. "One day, Emily Harrison…"

Emily's grin widened. "And I love you too," she quipped and then decided to bring out the big guns. "Come on, Mags, you know Barry's innocent and right now we are all that's standing in the way of the boy being charged with murder and spending the rest of his life in jail for two murders he didn't commit. We're the only ones who believe in him."

"Yeah, I guess so. It's just the more we interfere, the more people seem to end up dead. Maybe it's not an Alfred Hitchcock movie after all—maybe we've been dropped into a sinister Steven King novel and even the cars eat people in this town." Maggie let out another sigh and then sat up straighter in her seat. "At least while Barry's in jail, he's safe from the killer."

Emily nodded. "There is that."

Ahead they could see 'Joe and Jean's Truck-Stop Diner' and as the car drew closer, Maggie's eyes lit up and she leaned forward in her seat. "Hey, look at that," she said, her voice alive with excitement. "Someone's been busy since we were here last."

On the front window of the diner an artist had painted dinner plates the size of truck wheels. Dinner plates, covered in sausages, steak, chops, fried tomatoes, eggs and chips, all smothered in acres of ketchup.

"Oh, God. Food!" Maggie moaned and her stomach let out a long and loud growl of anticipation. "Breakfast at 6.30 this morning seems like several lifetimes ago. Let's stop here and buy a couple of hamburgers-with-the-lot-double-ketchup-to-go. We can eat them on the drive out to Mad Lucy's farm."

Emily stared at Maggie in horror. "How can you possibly eat after what we saw back at the track?"

"Just because my eyes saw a dead body doesn't mean my stomach isn't operating as usual."

"*My* stomach is telling me right now it couldn't handle a piece of barley sugar let alone a hamburger-with-the-lot-double-ketchup." Emily pulled off the main road, drove into the diner's car park and eased the car in between a monster sixteen-wheeler and a battered gray ute with windows so dirty the owner must have 20/20 vision to see through them. She slid a glance at the alluring pictures now covering the diner's large front window and ran her tongue over her dry lips. "Well, maybe I'll just invest in a cookie and a coke."

"Bet you ten dollars you change your mind once you walk through the doors and those heavenly smells assault your nostrils and tempt your taste-buds," Maggie challenged.

Although scorching outside, the industrial strength refrigerated air-conditioner sent a chill through Emily and goose bumps quivered along her bare arms as she pushed through the front door of the diner and checked out its occupants.

The lunch crowd had been and gone. There were only seven people left. A burly guy in grey King Gee shorts and shirt eating a truck size meal, four children, all under the age of seven, milling around the front counter while their beleaguered mother settled the account, and a hard-faced woman, early fifties, dressed in dirty jeans tied up with twine, a flannel shirt and a battered cowboy hat. The woman was hunkered over at a table on the far side of the diner chewing on a steak like a dog on a bone.

It shouldn't take long to be served.

The moment the rowdy family funneled out the front door, Maggie hitched up the waist band of her skirt and marched toward the counter. "Hi there," she said to the pretty young girl behind the counter. "I'd like to order a hamburger-with-the-lot-double-ketchup, please."

"You weren't here last time we called in," butted in Emily as she watched the girl write Maggie's order on an order-pad. "Joe and Jean not around?"

The girl, barely old enough to be out of school uniform, flicked her long blonde hair as though it was a move she practiced regularly in front of the mirror and sniffed. "Both out," she whined. "And if one of them doesn't get back soon, my boyfriend, Rhys, will be like going to the beach without me. This is so unfair."

"Where's Joe and Jean gone?" said Emily, moving across to take a bottle of coke from the drinks' fridge.

"Like Jean had a dentist appointment. She took off a couple of hours ago, and then like two minutes after she left, Joe said he had to meet some guy and he'd be back in half an hour. And he's still not back." She glanced at her watch, gave her hair another flick and dropped her bottom lip. "Like what am I going to tell Rhys? He's already texted me like ten times and he said he'll go without me if I'm not at his place by three. It's almost that now and I was supposed to get off work at two."

"Been busy?" asked Emily, placing a five-dollar note on the counter along with her bottle of drink.

"It's been like total chaos for the last two hours," the drama queen continued, the decibels of her whine increasing with every word. "Quiet now, thank God—except for Mad Lucy over there. That cantankerous old bat's been complaining ever since she flew into the diner on her broomstick."

Emily felt a big smile coming on. Mad Lucy? Here in the diner? She snuck a wary peep over her shoulder, almost wilted under the dagger-like glare thrown back at her by the woman in question, then, just to be one hundred percent sure, whispered. "The woman in the shapeless cowboy hat and a hunk of rope tied around her middle, gnawing on a piece of steak—that's Lucy Benham?"

"Yeah, that's her." The girl took several coins from the cash register and counted out Emily's change from her drink. "Old bat yelled at me when I served her, like accused me of burning her steak. And honestly, all I did was hold the meat over the griller for like *five* seconds. I swear *blood* was still dripping from the meat when I served her." She rolled her eyes and did her signature head flick. "I wouldn't be surprised if that woman's half vampire."

"Probably not." Emily let out a chuckle. "Vampires normally turn to charred ash in the light of day. Or, so I've heard." She caught Maggie's eye and grinned. "Mad Lucy's here in the diner."

"So, we either confront a vampire in a diner or a loose-triggered mountain woman on her own territory. Not much of a choice there." Maggie glanced across at the woman who sat at the table over by the far wall, both hands wrapped around a piece of steak the size of a family pizza. Caught in the act of ripping meat off the bone with her teeth, the woman bared her fangs and snarled. Maggie quickly looked away and shivered. "I've a hunch our contact isn't going to talk to us until she's cleaned up that carcass, bones and all. Reminds me of a dog I once owned. No-one dared go near him while he was eating either."

Undeterred, Emily towed her reluctant friend toward the woman who could have been a younger version of Grandma Clampet from the old 50's series, *Beverley Hillbillies*. "Come on, Mags, let's go and join our new friend. After all, we have as much right to eat our meal at her table as anywhere else in the diner." Noting the doubt on Maggie's face, she quickly added, "at least Mad Lucy won't shoot at us. Not with witnesses."

"I wouldn't count on it."

As they approached the table Emily dredged up her friendliest smile. "Good afternoon, Mrs. Benham. Mind if we sit here?" Without waiting for a reply Emily dragged out a chair and lowered herself onto the hard plastic seat. "We came over to offer our deepest condolences. You must be totally devastated about losing your husband."

But not devastated enough to affect your appetite…

The woman they called Mad Lucy lifted her head and Emily could see smears of blood around her lips. As she watched, Emily swore Lucy's eyes turned from brown to a hard dangerous black. Her lizard's tongue flicked out three times and then she slowly, carefully, licked the blood from around her mouth. Oh God, maybe the girl behind the counter was right and this woman *was* a vampire. Emily gulped but jammed her teeth together until they hurt. Even if Mad Lucy's head began to spin, which wouldn't surprise her in the least, Emily was determined to retain her smile.

"Huh," growled Lucy. "I've heard about you." She dropped the remains of her steak back onto the plate and wiped her greasy fingers down the front of her faded checkered shirt. "You're the two snoops who've been stickin' their noses into town business."

"No, no, you've heard wrong," said Emily in a soothing voice, the one she used on intractable equine patients before jabbing a needle into their backside and sending them to sleep so she could start work on saving their lives. "Maggie and I were just wondering how you're coping and if there's anything we can do." She turned to Maggie who appeared to be fascinated by the pool of blood on Lucy's plate. When Maggie didn't respond she gave her a sharp kick in the ankle under cover of the table. "Haven't we, Mags?"

"We have?" Maggie yelped, turned the startled exclamation into a cough and then smoothed her face into one of alertness. "Oh yes, we have. Definitely. Umm…like what have you been doing this afternoon to keep your mind from dwelling on your loss?"

"Not that it's any of your damn business but Craig's demise was no loss to me. Only stayed with the smarmy two-timer because I didn't want to lose the farm. Whoever popped the mongrel off did me a favor. As everyone in this town knows, my husband and I couldn't stand the sight of each other. Not that that fact was any excuse for certain women playing hide-the-sausage with him."

Hide-the-sausage? Emily's mouth gaped and she almost swallowed her tongue. God, she hadn't heard that term used in years. Not since her Grandma Nelly died eleven years ago. While Emily spluttered and Maggie blinked, Lucy picked up a king-sized china mug and took a long drag of coffee before continuing. "So…you can stop with your fake commiserations and get to the point. No, I didn't kill Craig—even though I was sorely tempted every time I heard of another of his pathetic conquests—so I guess you'll have to look elsewhere."

"What about John Taylor?"

She pulled a face of disgust. "What about him?"

"Did you have any reason to er…pop *him* off?"

Lucy spluttered, sending a shower of coffee over the table cloth. "Ape's *dead*? When? How?"

"About an hour ago. He was shot in the head—just like Craig."

Lucy Benham wiped coffee from her mouth and her face hardened. "Why the hell would *I* want to pop the dirty mongrel off? Just because he was a slimy bully who'd knock his own mother around was no skin off my nose. Hell, last I heard there was a line a mile long waiting to beat the guy to a pulp. He was a slimy—" she seemed to stop herself in mid-rant and her shoulders slumped. "But like my Craig—he didn't deserve to be murdered."

28

Rocky V — Ten Rounds at the Diner

Lucy Benham looked genuinely upset. Well, as upset as a woman who had returned to gnawing on a hunk of steak could look. Aware of the woman's distress, Emily reached across the table intending to place a sympathetic hand on her shoulder. But the way Lucy's fangs were chomping down on that half-raw piece of meat, Emily was afraid her hand might disappear inside the woman's cavernous mouth, never to be seen again. She snatched her hand back and tucked it out of sight under the table.

It was time to pick up Maggie's jumbo hamburger from the front counter and get going. Emily couldn't see any sense in hanging around the diner any longer. After all, Mad Lucy wasn't going to cooperate and there was still Charles Norton-Phillips to visit. That mysterious ten thousand dollars was a good motive for murder. Plus Emily figured it might pay to call in at the local dentist and check if Jean, the proprietor of the diner, and Ape's latest conquest, was *really* spitting out drool in his oversized wind-up fake-leather chair.

Eager to do more investigating, Emily scraped her chair back, stood up and looked down at her friend who seemed mesmerized as she watched Lucy's sharp fangs tear into the last of her steak. "Come on Mags, let's collect your hamburger."

At that moment the front door opened with a whoosh of hot air and Jean herself scuttled in, her sweaty face the color of a fire hydrant.

"Sorry, I'm late, Danni," she said to the young hair-flicker behind the counter. "The dentist took forever and then on the way home I had car trouble and the battery on my phone died and—".

"Yeah! Yeah! And all that time I've been left running the diner on my own." Danni, definitely not the sympathetic type, shrugged out of her apron that read BIG FOOD FOR BIG APPETITES and flung it on the counter.

"What? You're here on your own?" Jean wiped the sweat from her eyes and frowned. "Where's Joe?"

"I dunno, do I? He took off straight after you. Says to me like he'd be gone half an hour and he's still not back. Anyway, I'm off or I'm like going to miss out on going to the beach with my boyfriend," she told Jean as she made a dash toward the front door. "Tell Joe he owes me extra money this week."

"Don't worry, Danni, I'll make sure you're not out of pocket." Jean picked up the crumpled apron, shook out the creases and slipped it on over her head. "And thanks for taking over."

Tying the apron strings behind her back, Jean glanced around the diner and on sighting the woman in the cowboy hat with the remains of a bloody steak gracing her plate, the color drained from her face. "Lucy?" she croaked. "What are you doing here? I—" she said and grabbed the counter with one hand as though to stop herself from falling.

Steak forgotten, Lucy stood up, her body a coiled spring. "Well, well, well. If it isn't little Jean Bartolli, Craig's most pathetic conquest of all. I've been sitting here waiting for you." Her voice, crawling with menace, made Emily thankful Lucy hadn't been waiting for *her*.

"Lucy, I—I'm so sorry about Craig."

"I bet you are," Lucy snarled and crept two paces forward, a panther on the prowl. "Admit it, Jean. *My* Craig rejected you so you shot him."

"Whaaat?" Jean's grip tightened on the counter. "You're mad! I didn't kill Craig. I—I loved him. He and I planned to go away together. Leave this god-forsaken hole and start afresh in Adelaide."

"Bah. You hated the fact that Craig rejected you, so you shot him with your husband's rifle then tried to implicate him as the murderer." Her laugh sent chills running up and down Emily's spine and she could see Maggie's shoulders tense. "Craig didn't love you. Didn't know the meaning of the word." Lucy laughed and the chills increased. "He used to tell me what a great lay you were and how he got off on the fact that he was fucking his best mate's wife. But he'd had enough of you. The morning Craig was killed he told me he'd been trying for weeks to break it off, but you just kept clinging on like a bloated tick. God, he was already in another woman's pants by then and you were an embarrassment to him."

Holy Toledo! Emily blinked and she saw Maggie's mouth open like a trapdoor. If a producer was looking for a small-town in which to set a raunchy Days of Our Lives soapy, this town would make the show a Gold Logie winner

With a wild scream Jean let go of the counter and hurled herself at Lucy. "You're lying! It was you! You shot him! Craig loved me and was going to leave you, so you killed him."

Jean's right fist snaked out but Lucy easily dodged the blow, grabbed Jean by the hair and hauled her closer. "Listen up toots," she snarled, a drop of blood transferring from her lips to Jean's upturned face. "You're not the first air-head to be taken in by my husband's lies. He told that pathetic story to all his gullible conquests. What makes you think you're so special?"

"Nooo!" Jean wailed. "You're lying. Craig and I were running away together."

"Oh, grow up, Jean. Craig found himself a new flavor of the month so he broke up with you. Did he give you his standard line and tell you he couldn't leave his poor wife because she was mentally ill and he had to care of her? Is that what he told you, Jean?" She laughed and the laugh had as much humor as a snake's hiss. Is that why you killed him?"

Jean's reply was to throw a punch that connected with her opponent's nose. With an angry yelp, Lucy let go of Jean's hair to grab at her bleeding nose and then retaliated with a roundhouse uppercut that almost lifted the smaller woman off her feet.

Emily glanced across at Maggie and rolled her eyes. Should they intervene or should they let the two women fight to the death?

Maggie slowly got to her feet with a sigh. She cricked her neck and loosened her shoulders. "Come on, Em. We'd better stop this before one of them kills the other."

Damn…looked like they were opting to get on board. Emily gritted her teeth. She never was much good at fisticuffs—more into verbal skirmishes. Far less blood and bruising involved.

As Emily took a step closer, she noticed a big guy sitting at a table by the window. He was soaking up the last of his gravy with a hunk of bread. Then, giving a loud burp, he lumbered to his feet. Thank goodness. Now they'd have some muscle on their side. But no, the driver of the shiny truck outside strolled straight past the brawling women without so much as a raised eyebrow. He tossed a handful of notes on the counter to pay for his food and continued on out the door.

"Ready?" said Maggie, straightening her shoulders.

Noooo! Emily nodded.

"Right, let's do it then." Maggie kicked off her shoes and cracked each knuckle individually. "You take the skinny one and I'll take my chances with Mad Lucy Benham. Don't get in the line of fire though, Em. Those punches look pretty lethal. Just drag them apart so we can talk sense into them."

Don't get in the line of fire?

Just drag them apart?

Sheesh! Emily, who hadn't been involved in a full-on physical brawl since the third grade, when Tommy Wilson was caught pinching chocolate biscuits from kids' lunch boxes, hers included, blew out a breath she didn't realize she'd been holding. What if she tried her stern voice, the one she used on her four-legged patients when they tried to bite her in the middle of an examination? Or maybe not. 'Behave yourselves or you won't get a slice of carrot' probably wouldn't go down as well with these two combatants.

She edged closer to the two screaming women and watched Maggie dive forward to subdue Lucy in a brilliantly executed head lock. Woohoo! Way to go, Maggie! Emily brought her hands up ready to applaud her friend and then realized it was now up to her to restrain Jean and pull her away from Lucy, instead of standing back enjoying the show while Jean took advantage of the opportunity and peppered Lucy with a barrage of bitch-slaps and puny punches.

"Emily," gasped Maggie, her face a strange shade of purple. "I could use some help here."

"Okay! Okay! I'm on it!" Moving toward Jean, Emily executed several one-two shadow-boxing steps like she'd seen Rocky Balboa perform in the movie they'd been dropped into and then growled low in her throat. "Okay, Jean, fight's over. Time to act like a grown-up."

When Jean ignored her warning and continued to slap at Lucy, every slap weaker than the last, Emily snagged her around the waist and pulled her away. She grinned at Maggie and shrugged one shoulder. "Easy, peasy!" she said and wrapped both arms around Jean who was leaning against her, puffing, gasping, like she was contemplating a heart attack.

Maggie, still holding the flailing Lucy, rolled her eyes as though to say: *Yeah, yeah! Especially as Jean is now so exhausted a kid of five could have taken her...*

Naturally Emily knew that, but her grin didn't waver. "Maybe now these two can sit down and discuss their differences like civilized ladies."

"What do you say, Lucy?" Maggie loosened the hold on her victim's throat a couple of notches so the woman could talk.

Lucy's answer was to kick backwards with one pointed boot and collect Maggie in the shin. Maggie let out a high-pitched curse but hung on. "Evidently not," she gasped through gritted teeth.

"What about you, Jean?" said Emily leaning forward and speaking into her captive's right ear. "Ready to say *Uncle*?"

"Only if *she* is."

"Looks like we have a stalemate." Maggie shook her head and hung onto Lucy like a leech. A squirming, cursing leech. "What now?"

But Emily didn't hear her.

That smell. That sickly sweet smell. With her head close to Jean and one arm wrapped around her waist, the woman's perfume invaded her nostrils. Oh God, it was the identical smell of cheap perfume she'd inhaled behind the starting barriers minutes before they'd found Ape's dead body.

"It *was* you…" Emily let go of Jean and stared at the woman, her heart beating at twice its normal speed. "You didn't go to the dentist while you were out today, did you, Jean? You went to the track."

Jean stared back, eyes wide, the fight between her and Lucy forgotten. "I-I don't know what you're talking about."

"*You're* the murderer. *You* shot John Taylor and somehow dragged him into one of the starting stalls. Or did you get him to go in there first on some pretense at sabotage and *then* when he couldn't defend himself, put the gun to his head and pull the trigger?"

"No, no, you've got it all wrong, I—"

"It's no good protesting," Emily broke in, shaking her head as she pulled her mobile from her pocket to inform the police. "Your perfume gave you away. You were there this afternoon, at the back of the starting barriers—exactly where John Taylor was murdered."

29

A Close Call

Jean Bartolli? The murderer?

Maggie loosened her hold around Lucy Benham's neck, stepped away from the suspected-vampire-cum-madwoman and leaned against the counter. Or was that sagged? After restraining said madwoman, who was responsible for at least four of the bruises on her shins, her energy was way down there with the common garden-variety snail.

And now Emily had proof that Jean was the murderer.

Maggie shook her head to clear the confusion. Yes, she remembered the sweet smell behind the barrier stalls, but at the time, the sight of Ape's lifeless body tumbling out from behind barrier two and landing at her feet had blown the safety fuse in her brain and completely wiped the recollection from her memory banks.

She stared at the accused woman who'd crumpled onto a chair, tears sliding down her cheeks. Beside her, even Lucy was still, a look of shock replacing the earlier fury.

"Jean?" Lucy's voice broke the silence. "Is the vet woman right?" When Jean didn't answer, merely sat frozen on the chair, Lucy continued. "But why? Why would you kill Ape? Did *he* reject you too?"

"No, no," Jean cried, jumping to her feet. "You've got it all wrong. I didn't murder anyone. All I did was pay Craig and Ape five thousand dollars each to sabotage the track." She wiped her nose on the back of her hand. "Don't you see? The track was all my husband ever cared about. Never me. And I was sick of it. Closing the track down was going to be my farewell present to him when I left with Craig." Sniffling, she shook her head. "But I didn't kill them." She turned to Emily. "Yes, I was at the track today, and yes, I was behind the barrier stalls. But when I left, John Taylor was still very much alive. All I did was hand over another wad of cash to ensure the barrier stalls were inoperable for the opening of the races tomorrow."

"You can tell that story to the police," said Emily, opening her mobile and keying in a three-digit number. "They've got young Barry in custody for a crime he didn't commit."

"But I didn't–"

"Drop that phone!" A loud grating voice, laced with menace, came from behind them.

Slowly Maggie swiveled around to find a large man turning the Open sign on the front door to Closed. Heart in mouth, she watched him lock the door with a large key and pull down the blinds. "Joe?" Maggie's throat felt drier than sandpaper left out in the sun. What the hell was going on here? Every time they discovered the identity of the murderer—someone else put their hand up for it.

This time, it was big Joe Bartolli, Jean's snarly husband, co-proprietor of the diner and supposedly Craig Benham's best friend. And to seal the deal he had a very convincing black gun trained at Emily's head.

"I said, drop the phone, bitch or I'll blow ya head off."

Emily's eyes grew round and her face went two shades paler. Then, like it had morphed into a giant tarantula, she tossed her phone on the floor and stepped away.

Maggie, eyes on the phone, licked her dry lips. Maybe Emily had got through to the police. Maybe the police were on the other end of the line and could hear what was going on.

Gun still aimed at Emily, Joe marched across the room and with the heel of his size 12 boot, stomped the phone into what looked like a trillion pieces.

Maggie sighed. Okay, no police…

What now? What would Greg tell her to do if he was here? 'Cos no way did she want to die in this alien town. And what about her daughter? She couldn't leave Judy an orphan. Okay, keep Joe talking, that's what Greg would say. She licked her lips again and tried to find enough spit in her mouth to speak. "H-how long have you been standing there, Joe?"

"Long enough to hear my ever-loving wife confess to being the mastermind behind all the disruption at the track." His face contorted into an ugly sneer as he loomed over Jean, transferring his aim from Emily's left temple to somewhere around the middle of his wife's heart. "Don't you realize, you stupid cow, that it's *your* fault I killed Craig and Ape?"

"I-I didn't mean…"

"Not only were you screwing my best mate and that hairy baboon, John Taylor, but also paying them to stuff up the track so I couldn't race there." He stabbed Jean in the chest with his gun.

"Please, Joe, don't …"

"Because of you, I caught Craig, and then Ape in the act of wrecking my beautiful track. I couldn't let them get away with it, could I?" Joe seemed to go into himself as though his mind was back at the crime scene. "You know, I trusted Craig with my life. He was my best mate. And yet, when I was coming home from shooting rabbits in the early hours of Thursday morning I found my supposed best mate smashing up our new starting barriers. Couldn't believe it. And when I had a go at him, he laughed at me. Told me I was a loser and my wife had great tits and he loved kissing the butterfly tattoo on her ass." Joe's eyes cut to Jean and his mouth hardened into a cruel smile. "But I had the last laugh, didn't I?" He twisted the gun in Jean's chest until she screamed. "I shot the smirk off that back-stabbing traitor's face, tossed what was left of him in the back of the refrigerated van, drove to Port Augusta to pick up a meat order and when I came back, I stashed him in the ladies' restroom. That way, I wasn't here the morning Craig was killed, I was on my way to Port Augusta. So, how could the police pin his murder on me?"

Maggie stared at the man. He seemed so proud of his handiwork.

Joe slowly turned and glared at Maggie, his eyes black pools of darkness that had lost all rational thinking. "But of course *you*, ya stupid fat cow, found him, didn't ya? Had to go sneaking a look to see who was in the next cubicle. You're *sick*, you are." His snarl turned Maggie's legs into two sagging rubber bands. "Of course then I couldn't take the body out into the bush when it got dark and bury it like I'd planned." He poked Maggie with the gun. "All! Your! Fault!"

Finished with terrorizing Maggie for the moment, Joe turned his wild eyes back on his cowering wife. Oh God! Maggie let out the breath she'd been holding and wrapped her arms around her chest. This man was going to kill them all and then probably turn the gun on himself.

"And you," said Joe shoving his wife so hard she reeled backwards and slammed into the counter next to Maggie. "Not content with screwing Craig behind my back, you also got into Ape's pants and talked him into trashing the equipment at the track too, didn't you?" His eyes were colder than winter-frost. "See, I followed you today. I saw you give that hairy gorilla money. So, when you left, I stayed behind to see what he was up to. Soon found out, didn't I?" He shook his head. "You were scraping the bottom of the barrel having it off with that baboon. Made me want to puke, seeing you and him in a lip-lock with him grabbing at your ass. But what pissed me off the most was you paid the mongrels with *my* money!"

"It's not just your money," wailed Jean, face bright red, "it's mine too. I work harder than you in the diner. I'm here almost 24/7 while you're always off somewhere playing racehorse trainer or bending your elbow and laughing at dirty jokes with your cronies down the pub."

"You pathetic bitch! Ya never did understand me." He slammed Jean across the face with the gun so hard she fell to the ground, blood oozing from her nose.

"No need for that!" Maggie shouted and bent down to check on Jean who lay without moving on the floor, blood pooling down the front of her apron.

"No need for this either, I suppose," said Joe, and before Maggie could duck he let fly at her head with the toe of his work boot and sent her sprawling on the ground beside Jean. Then he quickly spun around and pointed the gun at Emily and Lucy who'd both crept closer.

"Get back!" he snarled, more wild dingo than human. "Now, we're all going to walk quietly into the back kitchen where no-one from outside can see us."

"And then?" croaked Emily.

"And then I'm going to dispose of you." His voice was so matter-of-fact he may as well be talking about putting out the garbage bins.

Maggie lifted her head. Very slowly. Very painfully. Oh God, the three people standing in front of her seemed to be swaying and blurred and their voices came from a long way away. She gritted her teeth as the reality of the situation came back to her. Joe Bartolli was a murderer and within minutes he would add four more victims to his total. Okay, the lump on her head hurt like a bitch and she felt disorientated but if she lay here like a log waiting for Joe to either drag her and the others into the back room and shoot them or even dispose of her where she lay, she'd never see her gorgeous horse-mad daughter again.

Blinking the dizziness away, Maggie forced herself to recollect the moves Greg had taught her if she was ever knocked down by a mugger, or in this case, a murderer. The moves she'd almost applied to Barry back at the track when she thought he was Ape. She glanced across at Jean who was either comatose or dead, blinked away the last of the recurring stars dancing in front of her eyes and took a deep breath.

While Joe's eyes were focused away from her, she had to bring him down. It was their only chance.

Maggie lifted her head higher and took in the dynamics of the room. Joe stood within touching distance, his back to her while Emily and Lucy, both with their hands in the air, stood beside the table facing Joe. She could hear his wild rant about shooting them and gritted her teeth in determination. Her eyes met Emily's and then she looked across at Lucy who winked at her. Holy bantam's eggs, Lucy Benham was even feistier than her little firecracker friend, Emily.

So…they'd both be ready to follow through.

"What if I scream loud enough for someone outside the diner to hear me?" threatened Emily and she took a step toward Joe, distracting him while Maggie shifted position.

"It'll be the last sound you ever make, vet lady," said Joe waving the gun in Emily's direction. "And what's more, I'll make sure the bullet doesn't kill you instantly. I'll shoot you where you'll bleed to death slowly. So slowly you'll…"

With one last push off the floor, Maggie wrapped both arms securely around Joe's knees, twisted and drove forward in the same action. Exactly how Greg had shown her. Whoosh! From her crouched position, eyes wide, breath caught in her throat, she watched the gun arc high in the air and land beside Emily's right foot. And then, almost in slow motion, Joe Bartolli, mouth open wide, toppled forward and crashed face-first onto the hard wooden floor.

In the silence that followed, all Maggie could hear was the deafening thunder of her heart beating a frantic tattoo against her chest. She'd done it. Thanks to her wise and wonderful husband's training, she'd brought the murderer down.

Both Emily and Lucy moved at the same time. Emily grabbed the gun and aimed it at their captive, while Lucy reached across the table for her truck-size porcelain plate, complete with the remains of her steak, eggs, and chips.

And then, with a loud ear-splitting, tally-ho, Lucy smashed the plate over Joe's head.

"Oh, my God!" whispered Emily, eyes wide as she looked at Lucy. "You've killed him."

"So," said Lucy, carefully spearing a piece of steak from Joe's bloody head and transferring it to her mouth.

Emily wrinkled her nose. "God, you are so disgusting."

"Mmm. Tasty," said Lucy, smacking her lips.

Maggie stood up and moved tentatively toward the big man sprawled on the floor. She poked him with her foot. No response.

Emily hovered nearby, gun at the ready. "Is he dead?"

Maggie, breath clogging her throat, bent down and inched her hand toward the man's neck, feeling for a pulse. "He's breathing," she whispered, afraid a noise might wake him up. "Guess it takes more than a plate to the head to kill this monster."

"Shame," growled Lucy. "What if I belt him over the head with the table? That might do the trick."

Maggie couldn't help the smile that found its way to her lips. Lucy Benham was madder than a snake caught in a trap but she was getting to like the woman more and more. "Maybe just tie him up while I ring the police." Both hers and Emily's phones were history so she slipped her hand into Joe's pocket and relieved him of his mobile.

"Tie him up?" Emily looked around the diner and shook her head. "With what?" And then, eyes on Lucy, she stretched out one hand. "Okay, Lucy, hand over that dirty hunk of rope you've got tied around your middle."

Lucy growled and pulled back. "No way! This rope is the only thing keeping my pants up."

"Look, I haven't got time to tread on eggshells around you any more, Lucy Benham. Give me that rope. No grown woman uses a hunk of rope to keep her pants from falling down. Go buy yourself some decent clothes. I need it to tie up Joe."

Maggie, pocketing Joe's phone after contacting the police, closed her eyes and leaned up against the counter. They weren't out of the woods yet.

The silence that followed sent the hairs on the back of Maggie's neck twitching.

At last Lucy spoke. "You're a bit skinny and I reckon you'd fight like a girl," she said. "But, I kinda like you."

"You do?"

Maggie opened one eye to see the woman dressed as a tramp give Emily a friendly punch on the arm. Probably hurt like hell but Emily just gritted her teeth and smiled back.

"Yes, you've got spunk, vet lady. And so has your friend with the cool moves." Lucy untied the rope and passed it across to Emily, one hand holding up her trousers. "Here, take this."

"Thank you." Emily dug in her purse until she found a large safety pin and handed it to Lucy. "Use this for now," she said then bent down to tie Joe's hands behind his back. "But later today, I'm going to personally drive you to the nearest big department store, 'cos you and I are going shopping.'

"Me? Go shopping?" Lucy fastened the safety pin in her pants then took the gun from Emily's hand. She knelt beside Joe and shoved the gun so far in his ribs, when he woke up he'd have a bruise the size of Australia to ponder over.

"Yep, and after I finish choosing your new wardrobe, you'll be the hottest cougar in Kangaroo Downs."

"The hottest cougar in Kangaroo Downs?" Lucy repeated slowly as she stood up. "Hmm…I like the sound of that. Ya reckon I could get away with one of them skimpy mini-skirts?"

Maggie grabbed a tea-towel from the counter and shook her head. "For goodness sake," she growled and knelt on the floor to tie Joe's feet together. "Could you two stop with the fashion exchange until after the police take Joe away? What if he wakes up and goes berserk? We need to stay alert."

Mad Lucy's grin was pure evil as she waved the gun in the air. "Just let him try. All he has to do is move a muscle. Just one muscle…"

Maggie looked across at Emily, sitting on a chair now, legs crossed at the knees, clean shiny hair styled in a face-enhancing bob, clothes from the top end of town. She cut her gaze across to Lucy. Snarl on her face, wild hair that invited passing birds to build their nest, clothes that scarecrows would reject. Chalk and cheese. And then, without warning, the alien image of petite Emily Harrison and manly Lucy Benham shopping at the Mall together, trying on panty thongs and teddies, discussing the merits of a body-hugging mini-skirt as opposed to something a little more elegant, flitted into Maggie's head. She felt a giggle bubble from inside.

"You two…" she gasped, "shopping at the Mall together…" A wild whoop of laughter almost brought her to her knees as she staggered to the nearest chair.

Emily grinned across at Lucy. Lucy narrowed her eyes at Emily and then ran one hand through the tangles in her hair before bending down to rescue her cowboy hat which lay upended under one of the tables. She studied Emily's clothes and then looked down at her own mud-caked boots and bush pants, held up with a safety pin. "Yeah," she drawled and wiggled her eyebrows up and down. "Shopping at the Mall together should be *real* interesting." The laugh that followed seemed to begin low in Lucy's stomach and by the time it burst from her open mouth was deafening enough to scare baby spiders back into their eggs.

When two police cars, lights blinking and sirens blaring, squealed into the diner's car park and six policemen crashed through the doors of the diner two minutes later, they found the proprietor on the floor, secured with a dirty hunk of rope and a tea-towel, and three hysterical women, arms around each other, hooting with laughter.

30

Kangaroo Downs Cup

Eight thoroughbred horses, sleek, athletic and beautiful, thundered toward them, a cloud of dust in their wake. It was the big race of the day—the Kangaroo Downs Cup. Emily, her white buttoned-up vet uniform over cool cotton pants and a colorful top, leaned forward in her deck chair to get a better view of the race. She could see the horses' muscles straining, their necks stretched forward and nostrils widening to inhale more air. How she loved to watch these beautiful animals in full flight.

The task of vetting today's runners had fallen on her and Maggie. The local vet, Emily's dark Heathcliff look-alike, was busy with a difficult foaling fifty miles away, plus there was a distressed alpaca in the opposite direction that had shredded itself on a barbed wire fence and needed the Doc's expertise with needle and thread.

On the chair beside her, Maggie, the egg-sized lump on her head forgotten, bounced up and down in excitement. "Come on, Big Ben," she yelled. "You can do it!"

Eight horses flashed by, jockeys crouched over their mounts' necks, silks a kaleidoscope of color against the cloudless sky. Big Ben, the rangy laid-back horse Emily had rescued by taking a bucket off his foot at Joe and Jean's Diner, hit the front with fifty meters to go and then powered away from the field. Emily was surprised the horse was even running today. With his owner/trainer, Joe Bartolli in jail, she thought the horse would be scratched.

"He won! Big Ben won!" yelled Maggie and stood up to dance a jig. Emily smiled. With her legs kicking in the air and grin a mile wide, no-one would imagine Maggie Post had brought down a mentally deranged killer less than twenty hours ago, sustaining a lump the size of a peacock's egg on her head in the process.

"Good afternoon, ladies," said a familiar pompous voice behind them. "Are you ready to present the cup to the winner?"

It was the club secretary, Charles Norton-Phillips, complete with a smart strawberry colored vest that strained at the buttons and a matching red and white polka dot bow tie.

"Good afternoon, Charlie." Maggie grinned at the secretary. "Did you put a few dollars on the winner?"

"The name is Charles. And why would I want a horse owned by a murderer to win our prestigious cup?" he snapped.

Emily flicked hair from her eyes and sauntered closer to Charles until her nose was almost buried in his colorful bow tie. "You know what, Charlie," she said and leant her head back a little so she could stare him in the eyes. "Funnily enough, for a while there I had the bizarre idea *you* were our murderer. Especially when Ape demanded you pay him ten thousand dollars. Why was Ape blackmailing you, Charlie? Did he find out why you can afford to buy a luxury car and do renovations to your home while the company you work for is going down the gurgler?"

"Whaaat?"

"I think you heard her, Charles. She's saying dirty little pots shouldn't be calling kettles black."

"Thank you, Maggie. I couldn't have encapsulated it better myself." Emily shook her head at the bug-eyed secretary. "Only two ways you could manage that, Charlie. And both ways point to you being a common thief."

Charles Norton-Phillips went white. It was as though all blood had leached from his face.

"Of course if I ring up, in say a month's time and find all that money has been returned, I mightn't go to the police. What do you say, Maggie?"

"I say, if that money *isn't* returned, there's a cozy cell next to Joe that comes with a ticked pillow all plumped up ready and waiting for a certain embezzler with a penchant for colorful bow-ties, to sleep on."

Charles reeled backwards, his feet clumsy in his desire to get away. "I-I'll just g-get the t-trophy from my office." He whipped around, almost fell, and then staggered in the direction of Administration.

"I think that went well," said Maggie.

"Put it there, buddy." Emily held up one hand for a high-five. "Even if we don't have a shred of evidence."

Maggie let out a laugh. "At least it'll give the weasel something to stew over for the next four weeks."

"Well," said Emily, slipping out of her vet's uniform and smoothing down the front of her silky top, "let's go present this trophy. And while we're there, I'd like to give Big Ben a congratulatory pat. Didn't think the big ugly horse had it in him." She laughed. "I suppose he'll go home after the races and brag about winning to his mate, Goat."

As they strolled toward the presentation dais to award the cup, Emily found she couldn't stop smiling. Thanks to her best friend, Maggie, they'd survived what could have been their last day on earth…which was definitely smile-worthy…but now, being part of the atmosphere, the tremendous excitement of Opening Day at the track, her heart felt lighter than it had for months.

"Hey," she said and crooked one arm through Maggie's. "Guess we pulled it off after all."

"Pulled off what?" Maggie sent Emily a mock-frown as they strolled along, arm in arm. "I can't remember pulling off any bank robberies lately. But if we did, can you please remind me where we hid the loot?"

"Idiot." Emily used her elbow to dig Maggie in the ribs. "We proved *Vets2U* is a service that delivers on its promises—no matter the obstacles. We're a force to be reckoned with."

"We certainly are, and I'm proud of us." Maggie, the lump on her forehead an ugly blue-black color today, squeezed Emily's arm. "No thanks to a certain criminal element in this wacky town."

"A certain criminal element, which, thanks to your brilliant husband's insightful lessons on self-protection, is now in jail."

By the sudden quivering of Maggie's bottom lip, Emily realized what her unthinking words had done. Upset her best friend. Maggie was missing Greg so much the grief was always only a heartbeat away. Emily grabbed hold of her friend's arm and squeezed. "You know," she said, looking around for a distraction. "I can't get over the difference they've made to the track overnight."

Maggie sniffed and then gave Emily a watery smile indicating she knew exactly what her friend was up to and appreciated the concern. "Yeah, country folk sure know how to have a good time."

Around them, the Kangaroo Downs race track, once a dull wasteland, had morphed into a party on steroids. Overnight, a flamboyant display of bunting and flags and noise and crazy castles and hoopla stalls and children's rides and beautiful people dressed in large hats and food-stalls had appeared. There was even a band playing under the shade of a stringy bark tree, complete with a country singer dressed in nothing but fringing and knee length boots. Picnickers sprawled under trees, children screamed, laughed and played, while serious punters, some in traditional shorts and tank tops, others in their best suits, sat around discussing the form, wandered the betting ring hunting for odds, or streamed out of the bar to the running-rails every time the beginning of a race was announced over the loudspeaker.

"Have you heard whether Jean will be charged?" Emily asked as they came in sight of the dais.

"Pretty sure she will. After all, Jean was the mastermind behind the damage done to the track and inadvertently, the cause of all the ensuing tragedy," said Maggie. "Can't help feeling sorry for her though. No wonder she was bitter. Joe treated her like something nasty on the bottom of his shoe and it sounds like Craig rejected her too."

"Yeah. Guess it will be up to the judge."

They climbed the mobile steps onto the presentation dais, which had been set up beside the track near the winning post, and joined the dozen or so dignitaries, mostly dressed in shorts and shirts and Akubra hats. No dressy afternoon at Randwick here. After all, the sun was hot enough to barbecue sausages and the atmosphere invited fun and entertainment, not top hats and three-piece suits.

Familiar faces stood out in the crowd. Stella, from radio station 5PU, a fashionable silk jockey cap perched on her blonde head. Danni, from the diner, hand in hand with a mop-haired boy she guessed was Rhys, the beach-loving boyfriend. And Lola, their landlady, dressed in a flowing caftan and eating fairy floss on a stick. All smiling and waving at them.

"Holy cat-o-nine-tails! Will you take a look at that?" Maggie's nudge almost tipped Emily off the dais. "Is that who I think it is?"

Emily followed Maggie's pointing finger and let out a loud whoop. "Yes, it is! We swooped on a dress-shop first thing this morning and as from today, the captivating Lucy Benham is officially the town's sassiest cougar."

Mad Lucy, dressed in a soft cotton mini-dress, low at the front and caressing every one of her curves, grinned up at them. She performed a showy spin, and then held up one boot-clad foot to show them the height of the heels on her classy suede knee-highs.

Emily grinned and did a finger wave. "Isn't she something?"

"She sure is!" Maggie laughed and then gave an appreciative whistle as Lucy saluted them with one finger, tossed her newly styled hair over her shoulder and strutted off, swinging her booty with aplomb.

"Ladies and gentleman," boomed the best-dressed of the dignitaries, "I'd like to thank everyone for coming here today and ask our two hard-working lady veterinarians, Dr. Emily Harrison and Dr. Margaret Post, to present the inaugural Kangaroo Downs Cup to the new owner of the winner, Big Ben."

Emily and Maggie stepped forward. So did Tony Matthews, the

owner of Kangaroo Lodge, the trainer who'd given lectures with them at the workshop the day before. Emily smiled. The big rangy chestnut couldn't have ended up in a better home. She could picture him grazing in one of their irrigated paddocks, stretching out on a bed of straw in a large stable, or swimming in their horse-pool while Tony's daughter, Teena, read a book. "That was quick," she told Tony while helping Maggie lift the cup from the table. "You must have had your eye on him."

"Called in to the hospital to see Jean last night and did the deal." He grinned. "Recouped half my money today."

"Congratulations," Emily said as she and Maggie handed Tony the heavy silver cup. "But if you want to keep winning, go back and buy the goat that lives in the paddock with him. Goat is the secret to the big ugly chestnut's success."

Tony winked. "Thanks for the tip."

While Tony Matthews gave his acceptance speech, Maggie and Emily moved to the back of the dais to listen. The presentation of the Kangaroo Downs Cup was different to any Emily had experienced before. It was like the whole town had won the race. Almost everyone, including stall holders, members of the band, Mums, Dads, babies in pushers, and opposing horse trainers, crowded around the presentation area and cheered Tony on. They laughed at his jokes and clapped and whistled when he held the cup in the air.

Life was strange, thought Emily, taking in the hundreds of happy faces in the crowd. While an unknown murderer and saboteur hung like black clouds over the town, everyone was a suspect and she'd been debating whether to get into her car and leave. Now, wherever she looked, she could see smiling faces—most smiles directed their way. It was like Tinkerbelle had invaded a horror movie, waved her magic wand and changed all the mean black vultures into colorful tweeting canaries.

With a broad grin, Maggie elbowed her in the ribs and brought her out of her reverie with a start. "Hey, Em," she said and lifted one eyebrow. "Do you realize you haven't mentioned my grubby little brother's name for at least 48 hours?"

Emily blinked and shook her head. Maggie was right. She hadn't given Peter more than a few glancing thoughts since they'd arrived in Kangaroo Downs. And what's more, she felt lighter, happier, and more self-confident than she had in months. Well, well, well. Maybe she'd started to move on with her life after all.

At that moment, a face with more metal than an airplane hangar grinned up at her from the back of the crowd. In his hand, held high in the air and waving from side to side, he clutched a small silver cup. Beside her, Maggie laughed, gave a whoop. "It's Barry!" she yelled. "And his greyhound must have won at Port Augusta."

Could this day get any better?

About the Author

A former school teacher and greyhound trainer, June has always dreamed of being an author. She wrote her first full-length story (with chapters) when she was nine-years-old—'Donald McDonald in Texas'—a story involving a rather extraordinary boy who rode buck-jumpers in a rodeo. And when she penned her first murder mystery, 'Murder Behind Bars', it resulted in her fifth-grade teacher questioning her home life. ☺

Even now, in retirement, June's favorite place to be is sitting in front of her computer, making up stories.